Sign up for our newsletter to hear
about new and upcoming releases.

www.ylva-publishing.com

Laid
Bare

A COLLECTION OF
EROTIC LESBIAN STORIES

EDITED BY ASTRID OHLETZ AND JAE

TABLE OF CONTENTS

Introduction

INTRODUCTION

This is the third erotica anthology we've been working on as a team. Like with the first two, we had a lot of fun choosing and editing those amazing stories about women-loving women getting what they want.

Of course, you'll have to judge for yourself how well we've done in our selection. But really, what could go wrong with such a wonderful pool of authors that we had the privilege of working with?

We suggest that you go and find some place to yourself where you won't be disturbed for a while, curl up with these stories, and go find your own personal bliss.

We're pretty sure that you'll have as much fun as we did.

Astrid Ohletz & Jae

FLASHBANG

Lee Winter

Daily Sentinel reporter Lauren King might have spent over a year covering the outlandish parties of LA's rich and famous, but she had never experienced anything like this. Hell no.

In the center of the Pacific Grand Hollywood's Arctic-hued ballroom sat an enormous bed, upon which was arranged a half dozen A-list actresses, barely dressed in scraps of white, tapping away on their cell phones and sipping colorful cocktails.

An Icelandic girl band was on a corner stage, swaying and singing a quirky folk-pop repertoire, their faces barely visible above shaggy white coats. They looked like blue-haired polar bears.

"Radiator Fluid, ma'am?" asked a passing muscle-bound waiter wearing nothing but white boxers and suspenders. He offered her a noxious-looking yellowy-green drink with a white umbrella in it. He was on roller skates. White.

"Ah, I'll pass." Lauren winced. "I'd prefer not to drink my car."

He rolled off, and she turned to study the glitterati, their shiny cocktail outfits flashing under a dozen mirror balls.

She shook her head. Only a bunch of overindulged celebrities would think that a 600-person white party with 100-proof cocktails would be a great way to launch their fashion blog, Flashbang.

A *blog*, for God's sake.

"Appalling, isn't it?" a sotto voice murmured near her ear. Lauren turned to find her good friend by her side. Los Angeles's top publicist was a vision tonight, draped in white satin, like some Rubenesque goddess commanding a toga party. Her scarlet slash of lipstick matched her vivid red hair.

But Mariella Slater wasn't just any publicist. She had a reputation for genius and could turn any celebrity's worst indiscretion into a publicity triumph. Such as last week when bad-boy action star Jordan Klauss tossed his personalized, handmade rubber sex doll from an eighth-story apartment window. It landed, with shattering effect, on an elderly resident's BMW parked below.

Mariella had spun it to the breathless media as a "highly technical stunt rehearsal with a minor gravity malfunction." She praised the star's "unquenchable work ethic" and noted that the car owner had scored not only a new BMW but, most importantly, free tickets to Klauss's next movie. Which was called *Slammmer*—with three Ms. Coming to a theater near you this fall.

She was that good. Who else could induce every entertainment reporter from 278 publications worldwide to dutifully name the movie amid their sex-doll-scandal copy? And they all spelled it right.

Lauren glanced around the room. She knew from her VIP invitation that her larger-than-life friend was the mastermind behind tonight's eyeball-bleeding monstrosity. It's just that she couldn't believe it.

"Mariella?" Lauren asked, dazed. "What on earth? It's like end times—in Siberia. Without clothes."

"I know, I know. Problem was it was planning by committee," Mariella admitted. "Froesha wanted everything white. Emmanuelle insisted on the roller skates to add a 'kinetic frisson.' Heddy wanted topless hunky men, because, well, it's Heddy. Veronica's mechanic-turned-spiritual advisor wanted the car-themed cocktails. Et voilà." She snapped her fingers.

"And the bed?"

"Trisha's new water and air diet has made her too weak to mingle, and Heddy's got a permanent hangover. The others like the way they can keep their dresses from wrinkling by not actually moving. And Emmanuelle can't even do up her dress at the back, so that's why she's lying the way she is. Besides, they do look gorgeous in the photos. Anyway, sweetie, enough of my brilliance. Let's talk about you. I'm so glad you came."

She gave Lauren a breezy pair of air kisses.

"Well it's kinda my job, so…" Lauren shrugged. Her off-the-shoulder, midnight-blue cocktail dress—a second-hand-boutique find which suited both her athletic figure and threadbare budget—shimmered.

"Not for much longer," Mariella said. "Am I right in thinking this is the last party you'll ever have to cover before you head to DC? Then it's just dull reporting on dreary people with no fashion or financial sense?"

"Yep." Lauren was unable to hold back her delighted grin. It was only her dream since she was a girl. From Iowa to DC. *Hot damn*. And all it'd taken was the exclusive of the decade.

Mariella gave her an affectionate smile. "Anyone would think you're happy to leave behind our decadent land of shallow dreams."

Lauren's head bobbed adamantly.

"Hell yes. Sorry, Mari, I know you love this crazy place, but I can't wait. I'm blowing this popsicle stand in two weeks, eleven hours." She glanced at her watch. "And fourteen minutes—give or take."

Mariella laughed so hard that her arms, ringed with a riot of shiny bangles, jangled. "Speaking of popsicles, where is your frosty, world-scoop collaborator? Isn't Ayers here tonight?"

Lauren's heart sank at the reminder.

"Catherine finished up her *Sentinel* contract a month ago, so she's off the hook on the party beat. And no, I have no clue what's she's been up to. I'm not her minder, so how would I know?"

Okay, so that was more defensive than she'd meant it to be. But it was a sore point. They'd both been flat out packing for their new jobs that had come about from their joint exclusive. And then, two weeks ago, Catherine had disappeared to work out some logistical issues at her next post. The occasional text message had been all Lauren had heard from her. And while her head knew how hectic things were for Catherine, her heart preferred whimpering pathetically in the corner.

Not that she'd shared that with anyone. Besides, she couldn't, given that they hadn't told a soul they were dating. They hadn't even talked about telling anyone. It was on Lauren's to-do list. But right now she was becoming adept at slapping on a happy face and pretending not to care what her prickly, former arch-nemesis got up to.

It wasn't even that hard. Everyone just assumed they still couldn't stand each other. Well, *almost* everyone.

Mariella leaned closer and whispered conspiratorially, "Lauren, sweetie, I know something's changed between you two. I can practically taste it. You vibrate on a different frequency when she's around. You light up like a C-list actress near the paparazzi. Don't bother denying it. What do you take me for? A *studio* publicist?"

A stain rose up Lauren's cheeks. Damn, Mariella was good. She looked into her friend's perceptive blue eyes and huffed out a breath. Then she finally gave in.

"It's still…new," she confessed with a sigh. She folded her arms. "And I haven't seen Catherine in two weeks while she's getting her new office ready. It's driving me crazy."

She felt a blissful amount of relief in admitting that.

"Ah," Mariella said with a sympathetic nod, and then glanced over Lauren's shoulder. "Well, this should help." She waved a red talon toward the door.

Lauren's gaze followed the finger. There stood Catherine Ayers. Elegant, aloof, glorious. Lauren tried not to swallow her tongue, but hell, she was only human. Her lover was dressed in a pale-lemon cocktail dress with pearl drop earrings, her auburn hair coiled up. Tendrils curled around her ears, showing a tantalizing amount of neck.

Lauren watched, transfixed, as Catherine's sharp gaze swept the room. When their eyes met, Lauren exhaled shakily. Then grinned like a complete fool.

Mariella laughed. "I see I was right. So here's the CliffsNotes—Your sneaky, secret paramour asked me for a ticket tonight because she wanted to surprise you at your last LA reporting gig. Who am I to stand in the way of the infamous Caustic Queen?" She dropped her voice to a whisper. "Or deny the woman she so clearly loves?"

Lauren's head snapped around to stare at Mariella. That was another thing on her to-do list. Declarations of feelings beginning with the letter L. Well, she knew how she felt…but, oh God, was it *that* obvious?

Mariella patted her arm and winked.

"Now, hon, I know that face. Don't overthink it. Okay, go on, have fun. Mock us and our silly, plastic world, and get drunk on Radiator Fuel and Dipstick Daiquiris."

She gave her an engulfing hug. Lauren felt the bruising press of her studded bangles and the powerful jolt of her perfume.

"I *will* miss you," Mariella said with a dissatisfied huff. "Very much. You always spoke the truth in a town where everyone lies to your face. And you always let me rant about those horrid little sacks of hormones turning my hair gray. Now *there's* some sage advice—never, ever agree to promote a boy band. And don't forget me when you win that first Pulitzer."

Lauren gave her a fond squeeze. "Never. You're unforgettable. All the best on keeping your hell clients out of the tabloids."

"Don't I always? Now, I'm going before I get all sentimental and rue my unwaterproof mascara."

Mariella gave her a kiss on the cheek—a real one for the first time—then wiped her lipstick away affectionately. Lauren's heart caught as her friend slipped into the crowd with a loud, bangle-clanging wave.

Her attention was soon distracted as Catherine arrived at her side. The formidable ex-Washington bureau chief might once have been banished to LA's gossip-writing beat to serve time alongside Lauren, but it had never dulled her fierce intellect nor silenced her biting tongue.

And God she was stunning.

"Well, well, Lauren King, goat botherer and entertainment hack," Catherine greeted her with her usual cool expression. Her eyes, though, twinkled. "What a surprise seeing you here," she drawled.

Lauren groaned. "Are you ever going to let the goat thing go? It was one story, like, a hundred years ago."

"Unlikely. The ground's much too fertile." Catherine leaned forward to air-kiss her but hovered for longer, lips drifting over Lauren's cheek until the fine hairs leapt to attention. Lauren suppressed a shudder.

Catherine gave her a small, knowing smile and then stepped back.

They regarded each other.

"You look phenomenal tonight," Lauren said after a few beats, eyes tracing the fall of luxurious fabric. And damn, she really did. A girl's hands could get lost mapping out the stunning lines of her dress.

"Lauren," Catherine whispered against her ear lobe, "if you wish everyone in the room to know what we mean to each other, keep looking at me like a steak you could devour raw."

"Can't help it. You're a sight for sore eyes. It's been *way* too long."

"Only two weeks," Catherine said. But her intense gaze belied her words, roaming across Lauren's form. Her expression grew appreciative as she took in the dress which so effectively accentuated her curves.

"Have you been clothes shopping with your neighbor again?"

"Yep. Joshua said I was looking like 'a sad, bedraggled hobo.' Direct quote. *So…* you like?"

Lauren smoothed her hands down her flat stomach, enjoying the way her lover's eyes followed them closely. Catherine's gaze slid up to her toned arms and came to rest near the swell of her bust.

Catherine's gaze was burning as she tilted her head and said with deceptive softness, "I believe Marc Jacobs should pay you to wear his label."

"*That's* who I'm wearing?" Lauren asked feebly. Her mouth was suddenly dry. "Okay," she said with a squeak.

There was a soft snort. "How is it you could write about this surreal nonsense for an entire year and not retain a single designer name?"

"Just lucky, I guess." Lauren gave a chuckle. "Besides, I had other things to think about. Vital things."

Catherine's eyebrows lifted. "All I recall was you trying to needle me to the point of rage for twelve exasperating months."

"Yeah. Like I said—vital things." She grinned unrepentantly, and Catherine's lips twitched in amusement.

A roller-waiter slid up and offered them a platter of appetizers with an over-the-top flourish. Lauren sighed. *Was* everything *overproduced in this town?*

"Charcoaled carburetor ball?" he asked with a straight face.

Lauren studied the blackened crispy spheres. "Does it contain *pure* carburetor?"

He peered at her in confusion, then gave up and turned to Catherine. "Ma'am?"

"No car parts before nine," she said drolly.

He gave them both an unimpressed glare and rolled away.

"The madness of LA," Catherine said. "Can't say that I'll miss it."

"What? You won't miss anything at all? What about the waitstaff at restaurants who give you their resumes just on the off chance you're a big-shot producer? Or Velveteria—the Museum of Velvet Art? Sad furry clowns for the win! Tanning studios on every other corner? Come on!"

"Shocking, but no," Catherine said before pausing. "Perhaps...well, I think I'll feel sorry about leaving my home. It was a sanctuary in this frivolous hellhole. Tad's expressed an interest in renting it from me at 'struggling artist rates.' Which I take to mean that he'll pay me random sums of rent if and when he ever finds an acting job." She rolled her eyes. "But I will miss my place."

Lauren smirked. "Well a lot happened there, no wonder you're fond of it." She gave her eyebrows a suggestive waggle. "I particularly think the guest bathroom should have its own shrine."

Catherine exhaled, her cheeks reddening. "God, you're impossible."

"Yup." Lauren grinned, but then her mood dropped. "These last two weeks have been terrible. Did you know that?"

When Catherine's eyes gleamed a little too smugly, Lauren added, "I've had no one to tease or work my evil schemes on at VIP events. Everyone's narcissistic and as shallow as a butter dish. It's been boring as hell."

"Did you really only just notice how shallow this place is when I wasn't here?" Catherine's eyebrow slid up to a preposterous angle.

Lauren considered that. "Yeah," she said. "I really only did." She brightened. "So…you came back early? For me?"

Catherine flicked invisible lint off her dress. "Hmm. Well, it was either that or take up an offer from Joe Biden to discuss his vision for growing Delaware's agricultural sector. Even my tolerance levels aren't that high."

"Gee, thanks." Lauren scowled. "It was me or tractors?"

Catherine gave her a smirk. "It was a close call. By the way, I'm reliably informed that your replacement on *The Sentinel*, that blonde creature with the unironic side ponytail, is here tonight."

Lauren frowned, trying to follow the conversation. "Uh, so?"

"So, I may have informed her that she has to update the paper's website on your behalf tonight. Therefore," Catherine said as she studied her, "your services here are no longer required. At least, not in a professional capacity."

Lauren blinked. "What? Candy agreed? Just like that?"

Catherine's smile became positively feline.

"It won't take her more than fifteen minutes. And I may have couched it in terms of being a smart career move never to argue with me. Ms. Summers proved her IQ might actually be out of double digits by agreeing immediately. Now then, I came tonight because there is something I wish to urgently discuss with you."

"Oh?"

Catherine placed her hand on the small of Lauren's back and propelled her through the blinding whitescape, past the industry insiders, VIPs, and socialites downing their colorful concoctions, and beyond the bed of pretentious, *Flashbang*-blogging celebrities.

They came to a set of double doors with shutters covering the glass. Catherine opened it and pulled Lauren through, closing it behind them with a snick.

"What are you…?" Lauren stopped. They were on a balcony packed with pots of ornamental trees of various sizes and shapes. Lauren realized these were probably from the hotel's ballroom, but had been hidden here to make room for tonight's all-white event.

Catherine led the way, and they picked a path past the potted forest until they emerged at the front of the balcony, next to one of two facing concrete pillars that edged the area. Far below was the darkened, outdoor swimming pool. Beyond that lay the bright lights of LA.

Lauren glanced back toward the door but saw only trees. It was like being dropped into an instant jungle. Even the air smelled different, no longer having the constant, smoggy bite she'd become used to permeating the pores of LA.

She stared around her in wonder. Catherine smiled at her awed expression.

They could still hear the distant tinkling laughter and music from inside the ballroom and low murmurs of people on other balconies, out of sight, on the other sides of the pillars.

"Uh, what…?" Lauren began. "I mean, why—"

Catherine stepped inside her space and backed her against a pillar, a predatory glint in her eyes. "Why?" she asked. "Well, I would hate for your last LA event to be unmemorable."

"Oh, um, yeah," Lauren said, eyes wide. "That would be terrible."

"Mmm." Catherine traced her fingertips down her face, the barest grazing of tips across her skin.

Lauren swallowed.

Catherine's fingers floated back up to her hairline, then disappeared into her shoulder-length brown hair. She combed them down to Lauren's ears, tucking any loose strands behind them. Catherine breathed against the shell of Lauren's ear, the tip of her tongue sliding along its edge.

"Oh," Lauren said with a whimper, finally grasping what their "urgent discussion" was about.

"We have to be *very* quiet," Catherine warned, eyes half-lidded. Then she pushed her body firmly against Lauren's. Her lips were tantalizingly close but did not touch, staying just out of reach.

Lauren felt the softness of Catherine's delectable breasts and the press of her hips and muscled thighs. She could feel the heat radiating off her—so ironic for a woman famous for her icy edge. Right now she was searing hot.

Lauren shivered at the thought of Catherine being aroused, and her nipples hardened.

"Are you cold?" The honeyed timbre of her lover's voice made Lauren's stomach flutter.

Catherine's knowing gaze slid down to study the two hard knots now jutting out against the midnight-blue confinement of her dress.

Lauren flushed. Her brain was flailing too hard to articulate complete thoughts. Or any thoughts, for that matter. She shook her head mutely.

"You certainly *seem* cold," Catherine continued teasing softly. "If only we could warm you up somehow."

Lauren's chest rose and fell rapidly. "Warm? Uh...I..." Her cheeks grew even redder as her voice faded out.

Catherine smiled wickedly and skated her fingers across the top of Lauren's dress, which was a straight line of glossy, strapless satin. Lauren felt the faintest whisper of warmth as the fingertips strayed off the dress and to her chest. Catherine leaned closer, and her breath dusted across the bare expanse of skin. Then, achingly slowly, she lowered her mouth to Lauren's chest. Small, teasing puffs of warm air sent goose bumps rippling across her skin.

"Poor Lauren," Catherine said into her chest, her words dripping with promise, "suffering so much."

Catherine's head dipped lower. She blew across Lauren's aching, erect nipples and then pressed her mouth against one through the dark blue fabric.

The instant moist heat was explosive.

"Oh *fuck*!" Lauren's eyes widened.

"*Quiet*," Catherine murmured into her nipple. "*Not a sound.*"

Bolts of arousal shot through Lauren as she watched Catherine mouth her breasts, swapping between nipples, thoroughly wetting the satin with her tongue.

She bit her lip, desperate to stay quiet.

Catherine's head lifted. "Hmm. I'm not entirely sure that's getting the job done," she said, examining the darkening wet spots. "Perhaps more direct methods are required to warm you up?"

"D-direct?" Lauren said. "Um...you mean...you want to... *Here*?"

"That's exactly what I mean," Catherine said and tossed her a haughty look. Her dark eyes were filled with the promise of every gloriously, naughty deed Lauren could ever imagine. And probably a few she couldn't.

She gulped, making an odd, strangled noise that had never before come out of her mouth.

"*Quiet*," Catherine said again. It became like a murmured mantra as her hands slid down Lauren's dress. They skated to her waist and then drifted back up to her chest. "*Quiet.*" She whispered kisses along her collarbone and ran her tongue down Lauren's cleavage. "*So very quiet.*"

Then, without warning, she pulled away and wrenched down the bodice of Lauren's dress with both hands. Lauren's full, naked breasts bounced into sight.

Catherine gave a pleased hum at the lack of bra, as her scorching gaze studied her find. Her fingers lifted once more to run lazy circles around a coral-pink nipple. She flicked it, and they both watched as the swollen flesh puckered.

"Delightful." Catherine's voice was low to the point of gravelly. It was doing funny things to Lauren's insides.

Catherine's lips landed on the nearest bare nipple, and she scraped her tongue across it.

"Oh *God*," Lauren said.

Her lover's white teeth nipped and nibbled at the sensitive flesh, and Lauren's hips began to buck forward. She wondered if she looked as desperate as she felt.

"Feeling a little needy?"

Well, that answered that question.

The tongue laving her breast paused, and Catherine's head angled up. The gleam in her eyes was positively dangerous.

"*Please.*" Lauren gasped. Her hips bucked again. *God, did she have* any *self-control?*

"Please, what?" Catherine's nimble fingers reached for the mid-thigh hem of Lauren's dress and waited. "Was there something you wanted? Something you needed?"

"*Catherine,*" Lauren said in a whisper. She swallowed.

The air around them felt charged. She could smell arousal and a hint of Catherine's perfume and a sweet peatiness from the press of ornamental trees. Her nerve endings felt as though they were misfiring. Every part of her skin was hypersensitive. A hint of breeze felt almost painful. And whenever Catherine's tongue slid teasingly across her flesh, Lauren's center clenched, craving so much more.

The hands on Lauren's thighs were stroking now—firm, even motions that were sending electric jolts straight to her core. The vision of what lay ahead was Lauren's final undoing.

Catherine—*the* Catherine Ayers, all uptight, Boston elite, fancy pearls, and superior attitude—was about to fuck her up against a wall at Lauren's last LA party. It was so damned illicit. So...*oh hell*...so *wrong.*

"God yes," she moaned.

So right.

"*Quiet.*" The lips against her breast said as they curled into a smile.

Feathering fingertips reached high up the inside of Lauren's thighs, and her muscles trembled in anticipation. She wasn't sure she would be able to hold her own weight if Catherine kept up such torturous games.

"Please," she whispered again, not even bothering to hide her wantonness. "Please touch me. God, I've missed you."

Catherine responded instantly, and by the time her fingers reached their goal, having first detoured past every inch of soft skin along the way, Lauren's panties were a soaked mess.

Catherine rubbed Lauren's cleft, outlined against her sodden lingerie, and groaned approval against her neck. "Good," she said softly. "I'd hate to be the only one."

Lauren gasped at the implication and, stung into action, reached for her desperately, drawing up the lemon-colored designer dress pressed against her.

There was a small gasp, so soft that Lauren almost missed it. She loved the way Catherine's breathing changed the moment she touched her. She hooked the dress in her fingers, drawing it higher and higher, the tips of her fingers playing over the slipperiness of silk stocking under it.

She paused when she felt something unexpected. A pair of lacy bands? Catherine was wearing thigh-high stockings?

She glanced at the woman who was settled against her neck, dragging her teeth across the skin, nibbling possessively. Their eyes met, and there was no mistaking Catherine's desire. Her lips curled up into a cat-like, possessive smile that was part smirk, part power play.

Those teasing fingers between Lauren's legs did a mischievous twiddle, causing her thumb to bump against Lauren's clit, reminding her that they were still there.

Lauren groaned at the gush of moisture under those maddening fingers and tried to distract herself. But those twirling fingers were playing serious havoc with her concentration.

Two could play at this seduction. She shifted her hands higher up Catherine's thigh, farther up under Catherine's dress, and then paused in amazement. All she felt was Catherine's warm thighs and then... Even *more* warm skin. *Wet*, warm skin.

"Catherine? Did you forget to put something on this evening?"

"On the contrary," came the arch reply. "Forward planning is an essential skill. I thoroughly recommend it."

Lauren swallowed. Her fingers rubbed against the slippery skin, mapping out Catherine's petite tucks and folds, relishing how much heat and liquid she could feel.

"Oh," Catherine huffed near her ear in a voice that sounded uncharacteristically ragged. *"Inside.* Now. *Oh Christ."*

The plea was the most erotic sound Lauren had ever heard. She entered Catherine with two fingers, pushing inside the pulsing, obscenely wet heat, and set up a consistent rhythm. *In and out.*

A gasp.

A tremble.

In and out.

A soft hitch.

Lauren pressed her legs together, desperate not to come herself.

A small cry.

In and out.

It was the most alive Lauren had ever felt, these moments where she claimed as hers this beautiful woman. A woman that everyone dismissed as distant. Cold. Unfeeling.

If only they knew.

Catherine rocked herself against Lauren's hand, making pleas for *faster, more,* and *yes, there, oh, oh yes.*

Lauren loved the clenching sensation as Catherine's body pulled her fingers deeper, demanding more of her. Her heart pounded at having such an intimate experience, knowing that Catherine was as aroused as she was, as hot and frantic and needy, and even if she wanted to, she couldn't hide it anymore. There were no more games. Not when she was like this.

She pressed the base of her hand against Catherine's clit and almost unravelled on the spot as a low, primal moan filled the air—erotic and raw.

Lauren's fingers were soaked in Catherine's essence, and she revelled in the proof of the effect she had on this enigmatic woman.

Catherine's hand between Lauren's legs suddenly twitched back into life. Without a word, two fingers were inside her. Lauren squeezed her eyes closed at the overwhelming sensation, combined with the intoxicating sounds of slippery flesh being stroked.

A teasing thumb snicked across her clit, circling it, flicking it, torturing it. Lauren quivered and felt herself clench, and then Catherine's wicked lips were on her mouth.

Catherine usually kissed her as though she had all the time in the world. As though playing and kissing were the same thing, a way of showing her skills at arousing another. But this was new. She plundered her mouth. There was no trademark finesse. It was like she was drawing her life force from Lauren. It was desperate, frenzied and so, *so* damned hot. They tangled tongues, aroused by each other's soft moans as their fingers drove each other's desire higher and higher.

Lauren was nearing her tipping point as the pressure built. Curling, coiling blasts of ecstasy were starting to radiate out from her clit, and her brain had turned into a sloppy, euphoric mush.

The smell, the sounds, the taste of those lips. She pressed closer into Catherine, holding on, clinging to her.

To Lauren's surprise, Catherine succumbed first. She crashed against her, pinning her against the pillar, and surrendered with a low, long moan.

Lauren lived for this. Seeing the walls crash down that kept Catherine apart from the rest of the world. Seeing the distance vanish, the guarded look fall away and just honest vulnerability reflecting back from her icy blue eyes.

Sometimes Lauren wished she could freeze time to that heartbeat when Catherine came undone, the first twitch where all her fears and hopes were exposed. Almost close enough for Lauren to touch and smooth away like a tear.

Catherine's eyes fluttered closed as she bucked again. The lost, helpless cry was enough to unravel Lauren. When Catherine's fingers sought out her clit once more, she shuddered and came with punishing force, practically crushing the hand stroking her.

There was a moment's silence. Fingers still held by the other's warmth, pounding with staccato pulses.

Lauren didn't want it to end. She never did. And after two weeks apart, it felt even harder to let go.

She felt the loss of Catherine's fingers and, with great reluctance, slid her own out from beneath Catherine's dress. They straightened their own outfits a little sheepishly. Then Catherine pressed herself gently back into Lauren, arms wrapping around her, holding her. Tight.

It conveyed more emotion than she'd ever openly said out loud. Maybe Mariella was onto something? It was a thought to dissect at another time. She felt those teasing, naughty teeth scraping against her neck once more. A reminder of who Lauren had just been claimed by.

"Wow," Lauren exhaled. "*Never* leaving. This is perfect right here."

A smile twitched against her neck. "Then you would have to explain to your new editor that you're passing up a career-making opportunity in order to satisfy your lover over and over against the wall of the Pacific Grand."

"Sounds feasible."

They both laughed.

"Lauren?"

"Mmm."

"Why are the waiters on roller skates at this thing?"

"Not sure. I think it's Heddy's fault. Or Emmanuelle's? I lost track."

"Ah."

There was a lengthy silence, and then the arms around her gentled and stroked her back. "Lauren?"

"Mmm?"

"I missed you, too."

Lauren smiled and exhaled shakily against the head burrowed into her neck, knowing Catherine would never see her relief.

"I could tell," Lauren said lightly. "And I missed you more."

"Must you always argue with me?" Catherine asked curiously.

"Ha. You like me like this," Lauren told her, dropping a kiss on her temple.

"Sadly. It's clearly a madness." Catherine caught her eye and then kissed her thoroughly. She pulled back, studying her. "Although I could get very used to this kind of madness."

Lauren felt soothed and a little giddy. "Yeah." She grinned. "I know the feeling."

Lauren King might have spent over a year covering the outlandish parties of LA's rich and famous, but she had *never* experienced anything like this.

∽∾∾∽

If you enjoyed *Flashbang*, check out *The Red Files* and experience Lauren and Catherine's journey from arch rivals to lovers.

A Different View

Jess Lea

The problem wasn't that the dress was powder-blue organza.

Nor that it was strapless, with shimmering beads accentuating the bust and a frothy, ruffled train at the back. Nor that it came with matching sequined kitten heels, and a box of pins and a roll of gaffer tape sitting ominously beside it.

The problem was that Steph was contractually obliged to wear it. For a photo shoot in *Women's Life* magazine. And Steph would rather swim the English Channel with two broken legs than be photographed in this dress.

"This is a *coveted* opportunity, love," Evie insisted. It was the same thing she'd said the last two times a miserable Steph had called her about it this morning. "The previous time they did a celebrity spread was with the prime minister's wife! And no offence, but you're just a sportswoman. It's kind of a miracle to get this."

Steph groaned. "Um, all right." Despite being described by Evie's focus group as "too threatening" (read: large, brown, and tattooed), Steph had never found it easy to say no to people. "But isn't that magazine kind of…old?"

"Course it is, love. Young people don't buy magazines." Down the phone line, Steph could hear the click and whoosh as her agent lit up a cigarette. "But who cares? *Women's Life* is on display at every checkout counter of every supermarket, newsagent, and corner store around the country. It's in your dentist's waiting room, on your grandmother's coffee table… We need that kind of exposure. We want the average person waiting to buy their milk and bread to be asking themselves: 'Should I know her?' If we can nail this and lift your profile, those sponsorship dollars will come flowing in."

"Couldn't we do another courtside shoot instead?" Steph pleaded. When she'd been chosen for the Australian national team last year, the evening news had filmed one of their training sessions, and it hadn't been so bad.

She pictured Evie's compassionate smile.

"Steph, people need to see that you're a fully rounded young woman with an exciting-but-relatable life off the basketball court. It's time to celebrate your feminine side and have some fun!"

This all sounded very sinister.

"Don't look so worried, love," Evie crooned, as if she could see her. "We're letting you keep the dreadlocks, aren't we? And it won't be some dreary old-lady shoot. I haven't told you the most exciting part. They've got Rin Takahashi working for them now."

"Who?" Steph sank down on the bench in the changing room and held the phone away from her ear to reduce the impact of Evie's outraged squawk.

"Sweetie, *everyone* knows Rin Takahashi!"

"I don't."

"Ex-punk performance artist?" Evie prompted. "Gave it up when it got too mainstream? One of the edgiest, most important photographers of our time?"

"Nope. Sorry."

"Oh, you're hopeless." Evie clicked her tongue. "Listen, Rin has photographed *everything*, okay? Paris catwalks, the Brixton riots, the last Yangtze River dolphin right before it died. Remember that iconic shot of the tribal medicine man staring down a bulldozer in the Amazon? Or the front-page picture of that tennis player punching her abusive father right there on the court? That was all Rin's work!"

"Um, okay…"

"All you need to know about Rin is that she's brilliant." Evie paused. "Basically, if Andy Warhol had been a woman with actual talent, he would be Rin."

If she's so brilliant and cutting-edge, what's she doing working for a housewife's magazine?

But the main point was clear long before Evie stopped talking: Steph was going to do this thing, regardless of her own wishes, and be grateful for the opportunity. That sort of message had been so pounded into her over the years by so many coaches, sporting federations, agents, and sponsors that she'd learned to tune it out and play video games in her head instead.

But now, as she hung up and stared again at the dress in front of her, she wished she'd fought Evie harder. Seriously, if Rin had chosen this thing for Steph to wear, how good a photographer could she really be?

"Nobody told me there was going to be ink."

The very first words uttered to Steph by the supposedly legendary Rin Takahashi were spoken with a metallic New York snarl and a crooked finger for the make-up artist, who came scurrying over. Jerking her chin towards the thick, black tattooed bands that encircled Steph's biceps, Rin snapped, "I could have worked around these if you had texted me about them even this morning. Now you'll need to cover them up."

The other women muttered their apologies to Rin and glared at Steph as if she'd got the tatts done on purpose to inconvenience them. Steph, who still hadn't received so much as a *hello*, folded her unacceptable arms and set her jaw.

Rin certainly looked the part of a cool, edgy artist: She wore a tight black velvet suit with an oversized collar and cuffs in dazzling white. There were thick silver rings on her pale fingers and thick silver bolts through each earlobe. Her glossy black hair was scraped back tight, and a single white stripe cut through it like a lightning bolt. Even in her chunky, studded heels, Rin barely came up to Steph's shoulder.

She did not look happy. "Well, let's get on with this."

For the shoot, Rin had chosen the car park of a crumbling closed-down factory. Steph glanced around at the chain-link fences, potholes, and graffiti, and didn't think they would match the dress at all. Much as she didn't want to do this, she didn't want the photographs to look ugly either.

"Couldn't we take the pictures somewhere nice?" she suggested. "Like a garden?"

The look she got from Rin could have stripped paint. The photographer didn't bother replying, instead busying herself with the lighting and snapping at the stylist and assistant to fetch this, adjust that, and "move the hell out of the way! I can see your shadow!"

Well, what did Steph know about photography? She sometimes took pictures of her lap by mistake with her phone camera. But she hadn't known she was signing on to this. An icy wind whipped through the car park, raising goosebumps over her exposed skin and making her nipples ache. Rin soon was ordering her to walk back and forth, to look over her shoulder, and to trail the hem of the dress through the rubble and muck. (The rep from the magazine squeaked in high-pitched dismay about that, but another one of Rin's glares silenced her.) Then Steph was ordered to lean for what felt like hours against a wall where someone had scrawled *Martian pussy* in giant green letters, before she was then told to crouch down and stare into a dirty puddle. As she felt the dress straining dangerously across her hips and back,

Rin stalked around, a frown on her heart-shaped face, her heels kicking up mud as she barked out instructions to the stylist: "More powder—I can still see the shine! Tape that gaping neckline, it's not a porno! You gotta do something about that *hair*. It's killing me here!"

With each impatient shout, Steph felt her body—so fast, fit, and powerful most of the time—becoming lumpy, clumsy, and ugly. She was too tall, too hefty, too unfeminine. Jesus, it was like being back in high school.

A tiny leaf had landed in Steph's hair; Rin reached up without asking permission and flicked it away. Even though her fingertips touched the leaf only, Steph froze at the unexpected closeness. But Rin was already stepping back again.

"Right." Rin exhaled irritably. Every shot seemed to frustrate her more. "Up those stairs."

"You're kidding me." The outdoor stairs led to a boarded-up door two storeys high. They were so rusted and rickety Steph doubted they would take her weight.

"You've already kept me waiting for hours because 'walk a straight line' is apparently too hard for a jock to understand. You think I've got time to kid?"

"*Excuse me?*" She was used to sledging on the court—it was only natural your opponents would try to put you off your game—but what was this woman's problem? Weren't they supposed to be working *together*?

Rin rolled her eyes. "Oh, just climb the damn stairs!"

Steph managed five of them, trying to follow Rin's yelled instructions about leaning over the handrail ("I said moody, not constipated!"). But when she felt the sixth stair buckling beneath her, she refused to go further. It was bad enough trying to ignore the crowd of kids who were yelling things from the bus stop nearby. Her season contract didn't cover her for injuries off the court, not to mention this would be an embarrassing accident to explain to people.

"Hey, I'm sorry if your agent didn't tell you how this works!" Rin raised her voice over the wind that was now whistling across the factory grounds. "But this is my shoot, and you've agreed to follow my directions!"

"Well, I'm sorry if she didn't tell *you* how this works." Steph's teeth were starting to chatter from the cold as she clambered down. "But one accident can end my career. So, forget it."

Rin actually fell silent. Was she outraged, or just surprised? At last she said, "Fine, then. You can chuck some stones." Rin emptied a handful of gravel into Steph's palm, then dusted her own hands off and wiped them with sanitiser. "Think you can manage that?"

"Where do you want them?" *I know where I'd toss 'em*, she thought with a lethal glare. *Right into the lens of your fancy camera.*

But Rin pointed up at the highest shattered window of the abandoned factory. "Let's see you hit it."

When Steph managed it easily, Rin raised one tapered eyebrow. She might have even looked faintly impressed. She lifted her camera. "Do it again."

Steph obliged three more times, feeling the dress threatening to rip under her arm. Hitting her mark was easy, but she didn't like it. "You know, I don't think we should be vandalising buildings, especially when there's kids watching. Us players are supposed to be role models."

"Oh, for Chrissake." Rin's better mood hadn't taken long to evaporate. "Fine, you can walk through that pile of garbage if you'd prefer. And make sure to give it a good kick."

Steph stamped over, feeling more and more resentful as the wind screeched around her. Even her ears and nose were frozen, and her fingers were throbbing with cold. God knew what these bloody pictures would look like. She imagined an elegant middle-aged woman leafing through the magazine at the supermarket checkout, catching one glimpse of Steph, and throwing it back in disgust.

As the light worsened and a few spots of rain hit the concrete, Rin's instructions grew frenzied and shrill: "Lift your chin! Your left, not my left! For God's sake, *relax*!"

"Why does it have to look all dirty and ugly?" Steph couldn't help provoking her. "And why can't I smile?"

"What have you got to smile about?" Rin snorted. "You look like a rugby player at a drag night! I'm trying for irony here." She fiddled furiously with the camera. "Ill-fitting frivolity amidst urban decay. I wouldn't expect you to understand."

"What is your *deal*?" Steph's temper was rising fast.

"Oh, apart from freezing my ass off because you can't follow a few simple instructions?" Rin's voice had not been quiet this entire session, but now it seemed to rattle the broken windows.

"I'm doing what you told me to!"

"I said to act natural. You look like Robocop on his way to the prom!"

"Well, excuse me for not being a glamour model catwalk...person." Steph stumbled, then scowled. "But at least I'm good at my actual job." She cheered herself up for a moment by imagining Rin as a very puny opponent who could be sent flying by a well-timed shoulder charge. "You're the one who's meant to be some kind of genius at taking photos—which is not that friggin' important, by the way, even if you think it's better than brain surgery. So if the pictures are turning out crap, whose fault is that?"

Rin lowered the camera. Behind her designer spectacles, her black eyes glinted murderously.

"Maybe this boring, provincial, little desperate-housewives magazine, which can't think of anything better to do with my considerable talents than happy snaps of pathetically closeted B-grade athletes—to print in between cupcake recipes and tampon advertisements! Maybe it's their fault!"

Steph flinched at the "closeted" remark. The stylist had backed away by now; her assistant was hiding in the car. But Steph stepped forward. "You've got no reason to talk to me like that. In fact, you've been an arsehole from the word go. You think I want to be here doing this? If I've made some sacrifices, it's because I love what I do. If you don't even like your job and you think you're too good for it, why don't you get a better one and stop being such a bully?"

Rin's eyes widened, her face a mask of rage. The stylist ducked behind the car, fumbling for her keys as if to make a quick getaway. The wind howled with renewed force, whipping Steph's hair across her face.

Rin ripped the camera from around her neck. Steph got ready to dodge before slowly and with visibly forced calm, Rin lowered the instrument to her side. Holding Steph's gaze, she stepped forward, moving closer until Steph could see the tiny, delicate lines at the corners of her mouth and eyes, like the faintest of brushstrokes across Rin's pale skin.

"Oh, believe me, I wish I could." Rin's voice had contracted to a furious whisper. She pressed her narrow lips together as the camera shook in her hand. "If I'd stayed at *GN* magazine last year, I'd be at the top of my game by now. Do you know I had a whole project lined up with one of their reporters: inside life on a polygamous Mormon compound? Not to mention an exposé on juvenile prisons." She shook her head. "Back then, if anyone had suggested a shoot like this, I would have laughed in their face."

"Why aren't you there now, then?"

Rin exhaled hard through her nose, then slumped and ran a hand over her impeccable hair.

"A little incident with our biggest advertiser. Who went to college with our biggest shareholder. Not everyone agreed with how I handled it."

"What did you do? Tell *him* that his tattoos were 'literally giving you the worst migraine of your life'?"

"No." Rin hesitated. "I threw a bowl of shrimp salad at him."

Steph couldn't help gaping. "For real?"

Rin nodded.

"Why?"

Steph got a hard look in response. "Demanding blow jobs from frightened young interns doesn't play well with me." When Steph stared, Rin curled her lip. "You want to talk bullies? Some of these assholes are worse now than they were in the seventies." She looked away, across the scattered bricks and the puddles rippling with new drops of rain. "My own fault for getting too comfortable inside the capitalist machine. I thought I was in high enough demand that I could make my point and fuck the consequences. But it's true what they say: 'You can always be replaced.'" She took off her glasses and wiped the rain off them. "By the time those guys were through, I was damn near unemployable."

"Wow." Steph took that in. "All because of a bowl of salad?"

She cocked her head. "Well, there might have been a platter of sushi too. And a basket of zucchini vegan mini-muffins."

"Best use for zucchini muffins I can think of," Steph offered.

Rin gazed upwards. "And a trestle table."

"You did the right thing." Steph's weight shifted from foot to foot. "Well, sort of."

"No." Rin sighed. "A tray of shot glasses would have been way more rock-and-roll. Damn lunchtime launches."

A weary silence fell. The rain was settling in, spattering in fat, cold drops against Steph's face and pooling inside her sparkly shoes.

Rin sighed. "Oh, let's get out of here. The shots we've got will have to do."

"Sorry if the photos are no good," Steph mumbled. She picked up the sodden, grimy train of her dress in one fist and followed Rin to where their cars were parked.

"Oh, you were right." Rin shrugged. "It wasn't your fault."

"Well, I can't do dresses." Ten minutes before, there was no way Steph would have shown weakness in front of this scornful, bad-tempered woman, but now she heard herself say, "I've always looked awful in them. Even when I was a kid. You were kind of right about my high school formal, actually. It was, like, torture."

"Please." She waved a hand. "Naomi Campbell couldn't have done anything with that dress. It looks like someone threw up a blue Slurpee into Dolly Parton's purse."

"Yeah, it—" Steph tripped over her own sentence. "Hang on, you chose it!"

"*Me?*" Rin reeled, then, for the first time that afternoon, actually laughed. Up close, her slightly crooked front teeth made her look younger. "Honey, if you weren't half my age and twice my size, I'd slap you for that. The dress was a deal between the designer and the magazine—nothing to do with me."

"Really?"

"Hey, when I do bad taste, I do it well."

As they reached the car, Rin adjusted her square spectacles, then appraised Steph's top half: her broad, bare shoulders; her large hands; the black rings of her tattoos shimmering as the rain washed the concealer away. Steph looked down at Rin. There were drops of water sliding through her raven hair and beading on her velvet lapels.

"If I had my way," Rin said, "I wouldn't have shot you in that monstrosity. With the body you've got to work with… Well, let's say I wouldn't have hidden it under ten million ugly sequins."

A burst of surprised laughter escaped Steph's lips, and she looked away in embarrassment. But even as she did so, she felt a pleasurable heat rising in her cheeks.

"I don't know about that…" She hesitated, then to her own surprise she added, "But I'm heading to the gym now. If you want…" She glanced down at Rin's camera. "I mean, Evie wouldn't like it. And I guess it's not what the magazine wanted. But…"

The rain was coming harder now. Rin slid into the car without another word and yanked the door shut.

Crestfallen, Steph took a step back before her phone sounded in her bag.

There in 20, it read. *Text me the address.*

❧

Steph had only ever worked out in front of teammates, coaches, and personal trainers. But she'd been competitive right from the beginning, eager to impress, always wanting to be the one who could go faster, who could last longer.

"You come alive in front of an audience," her high school phys. ed. teacher had joked, and Steph, so shy and awkward outside of gym class, had grinned back.

Who knew all it would take to push her to the next level would be a short, cranky, fifty-something photographer in kinky shoes?

The Rin Takahashi who followed Steph into the gym was a different artist to the one who'd pushed her around in the factory lot, barking orders. Once they were in the weights room—with its pounding eighties rock; faded bodybuilding posters; and the smell of leather, sweat, and disinfectant—Rin was transformed.

Gone were the tantrums, the arrogance, the endless complaints. Now Rin watched in near silence through the camera's lens or over its neat black body. Her stance was relaxed, and there was a tiny smile on her face as Steph, now dressed in tight cotton shorts and a singlet, warmed up on the treadmill, then moved to the mat for push-ups and lunges. She stepped around Steph with careful movements and leaned against neighbouring benches and mats, out of her way but always present. Occasionally she would murmur some suggestion—"Turn your face a little?"

Steph felt her skin growing warm, her pulse stirring beneath her drowsy flesh. Her muscles, cold and stiff from those wasted hours outdoors, protested at first, but before long, she felt them lengthening, growing accustomed to the burn. Her heartbeat quickened. The camera blinked and whirred.

"I used to look down on sports photography," said Rin as Steph dropped to the mat for another ten push-ups. "Before I tried it, I mean."

"Oh yeah?" Steph paused in mid-air, feeling the muscles groaning pleasurably along her arms and shoulders. She lifted her face to smile at Rin.

"Yeah. I assumed it was some kind of pathetic wish fulfilment. You know, for the sort of nerdy kids who fantasised about hanging out with the athletes."

"Is that right?" Steph rose to her knees, noting with satisfaction the traces of her own sweat left shining on the mat.

Rin chuckled. "Well, it might be a little bit right, actually."

As Steph led the way to the weights area, she could feel perspiration trickling from her hairline down between her shoulder blades, making her singlet stick to the small of her back. She tugged the soaked fabric away from her skin and caught Rin watching.

"You know," said Rin, "we're almost by ourselves in here, and none of that lot are looking." She pointed to a lone group of men in the far corner, who seemed much more interested in each other's glutes than in Rin and Steph's photography session. "You could take that shirt off."

So Steph did.

In her sturdy black sports bra and tiny shorts, she moved onto the equipment: lat pull-downs, then bench presses. As her body hit its familiar rhythm, she closed her eyes, breathing out with each searing push of her muscles, then inhaling the tang of her own exertion, offset by puffs of chemical sweetness as her deodorant kicked in. She could feel the heat hammering in her temples, the perspiration sliding down between her breasts. She sensed Rin watching her and was determined not to disappoint, pushing herself on and on. The memories of the humiliating fashion shoot were fading fast. This was where Steph belonged, and she would show Rin what discipline looked like.

Only when her body was screaming for release did she let herself move on, over to the bench for a set of bicep curls.

"Happy with these shots?" she asked Rin in between rough breaths, the weight rising and falling in a steady rhythm.

"Not quite," said Rin from where she sat on the next bench. But she was smiling. She lowered her camera and leaned over, reaching around Steph's mighty arm where it was curled to her chest, the dumbbell steady in her hand. She stroked one stray lock back behind Steph's ear.

Rin's fingertips were soft.

"Now I'm happy," Rin said.

ᔕᕐᕑᐁ

That night, stretched out alone on the couch, Steph found her mind drifting back to that gym shoot. Usually she showered and changed as soon as she got home, but somehow tonight she preferred to stay in her shorts and bra that carried the vague scent of her workout and an enticing artificial spiciness that might have been Rin's perfume.

A women's rugby sevens replay was on, but for once, Steph couldn't concentrate. She shut her eyes, recalling how it had felt to impress Rin, a woman who acted like she'd seen it all before. She remembered the non-stop clicking of Rin's camera, capturing every crunch and release of her muscles, every heavy breath and bead of liquid that ran down from her temple.

And she'd done well, hadn't she? Gone harder than ever before? The lingering ache in her limbs, that delicious, well-earned exhaustion told her so. Absently, Steph ran her fingertips down her thick, sleek thighs, relishing the power that lay dormant there and the smooth warmth of her skin.

Her phone beeped. She picked it up to find a text.

Thanks for today. You were impressive.

Steph smiled.

My pleasure.

The phone sounded again.

The pleasure was mutual, then. And if I can persuade our boring editor to take a risk on a photo shoot, thousands of women might get to enjoy you too.

That made Steph laugh out loud.

Not sure about that.

There was a pause before the reply.

Oh, think about it. Bored, pampered rich lady drops off the kids, settles on the sun lounge with a Bloody Mary, opens her magazine—and sees this.

Rin had attached a photo: a close-up of Steph craned over on the bench, her face set in determination, her bicep swollen taut with effort, the weight curled to the level of her chin. Rin had altered the background so it lay in shadow; there was nothing in the picture but Steph herself. Her tattoos bulged, and her bare skin was gleaming.

"Woah," Steph whispered to the empty room and messaged back.

Some trick—looks incredible! WTF did you do?

She could almost hear Rin's odd, curt chuckle in the message.

No tricks. That's what you look like. My job is to weed out the mess and distractions so people can see what's there.

This time, there was only a brief pause.

Imagine how that picture might brighten up some suburban lady's afternoon—or change her life.

And Steph did find herself imagining it: some middle-aged woman with perfect hair, impeccable make-up, and designer sunglasses, wearing the sort of expensive activewear Steph usually despised. She'd be sitting poolside, flipping open a glossy page and expecting to find salad recipes and celebrity gossip—and instead stumbling across that picture. Steph pictured the woman lifting her shades, her eyes widening over the rim of her glass…

How about these?

One picture showed Steph at full tilt on the treadmill, arms pumping, dreadlocks flying. Her face was focused intently on some point in the distance. Her eyes were sharp, her nostrils flaring as she inhaled deeply. The next picture captured her in mid-push-up. The strength in her upper body that she'd worked to build every day since she turned twelve was unmistakable.

Steph stared at it for a long time. Okay, she'd known she was fit, but this…

Suddenly the stupid blue photo shoot dress, the dreadful pictures from her school formal, and a hundred other tiny humiliations throughout her youth were shown for what they were: irrelevant.

Amazing. Never thought I could look so good.

Rin's message shot back.

Why not?

Steph gazed at the photos again and then at a fourth one Rin had sent through. It showed Steph prone on the bench, bare legs braced, elbows bent as she drew the weight slowly and smoothly all the way down to her chest. Sweat was glistening across her bare belly and the tops of her breasts. Her lips were pursed as she exhaled.

Damn. Rin's words repeated inside her head: *Why not?*

Why wouldn't that woman sipping cocktails on her sun lounge pause to take a second look? Why wouldn't she study the contours of Steph's body, the fruits of such hard and dedicated training, and admire the determination on Steph's face? Why wouldn't she run the fingers of her free hand over one bare thigh as she examined the picture, gliding upward until she reached the seam of her shorts, now warmer and damper than usual?

Like Steph was doing now…

Steph slipped her fingers beneath the cotton to stroke the tender flesh at the very top of her thigh, tracing light circles with her middle finger while her thumb kept bumping against her clit. She was swollen and sensitised down there, tingling already.

Her phone flashed again.

And as for this…

Not many women could manage to do pull-ups on the gym's thick door frame, so when Rin had challenged her, how could Steph resist? The photo, taken from below, showed her round, firm arse at an angle she'd never seen before.

"Jesus…" The picture on Steph's phone did battle with the image in her head, of that horny rich woman now ogling this particular photo before sliding one hand, with its ruby-red nails and diamond rings, down beneath the waistband of her tight, white shorts. To soothe the need that throbbed below…

Steph's black cotton panties were shockingly wet. Had she really done that to herself so easily? Through the material, she gave her clit a tentative rub, then gasped at the intensity of her body's pleasure. Unable to wait, she lifted the elastic at her hips and thrust her hand inside.

She dug her first two fingers into her fleshy outer lips, massaging them slowly up and down before pausing to give her hair several firm, quick tugs, just the way she liked it.

Her body responded with a rush of heat that lifted her hips off the couch. She glanced back at her phone, swiping through the pics with her free hand, lingering over the startling beauty of her own face, of her almost-naked body. *Fuck, yes.* She slipped her fingers lower, between her more delicate and frilled inner lips. They were dripping.

Her phone sounded, startling her. Rin again.

You've gone quiet. Having fun?

Steph breathed out hard. How did she know? Or were the pictures really so hot that any woman might do the same? She imagined that haughty middle-aged woman again on her pool lounge, her drink now forgotten beside her. Imagined her licking her painted lips as she breathed faster over Steph's pictures, pausing to finger her nipples through her tight pink top, her hips jolting, her right hand busy between her elegant thighs.

Except now that woman was starting to look like Rin.

The phone wobbled in Steph's hand.

Mind your own business.

She yanked her shorts and underwear down her legs, parted her thighs, and slid a single questing finger up inside.

As if testing her strength against yet another weight, she breathed out slowly while the protective muscles clenched then relaxed to permit her entry. Damn, it felt so good: the roughness, the sponginess, and then her body's firm grip giving way to a hot, delicious friction.

Behind her closed eyes, the sexy socialite definitely looked like Rin now. And although Steph had resented Rin's orders that morning, now the two photo shoots merged in her head, and Steph imagined herself back at the gym, sweat pouring down her and Rin's voice snapping at her: *Harder! More weight! Get up, you're not done yet! Show me what you're made of!*

Her hand pushed and pumped, and she angled her finger upward to hit that sweet spot. Hot pulses of pleasure were reverberating down the backs of her thighs. Her phone flashed again. *Damnit*, she was almost—

Oh, really? So you won't want these, then?

Steph's eyes widened. She'd almost forgotten the outdoor session in the gym's battered old basketball court. The sight of herself in her element, spinning a ball on the tip of one finger to show off, was amazing. Rin had faded the background into a blur of concrete and metal, but every detail of Steph's figure was crystal clear: her joyful grin, the muscles standing out like ropes in her lean thighs, the silver butterfly stud in her left ear. In one picture, her powerful frame was crouched over the ball as she travelled it fast down the court; in another, Rin had captured Steph's figure in flight, both feet off the ground, one long arm stretched all the way to the hoop. God. She was magnificent.

Left-handed, she texted back.

Hell yes, I want them. Incredible.

It was as if Rin had already had her finger poised over the *send* button.

I could do better. Next time I'll go with an Olympian theme. You as the champion, naked in a laurel wreath. Spears and arrows and discus shots. Show off those guns properly. Would you do it?

Steph felt her face crack into a smile. She couldn't believe Rin was being so flirty, or that she was loving it so much. Slowly, she withdrew her slippery finger and strummed the very tip of her clit until it shot sparks right through her.

She texted back.

Naked? Sure you could handle that?

Then she jammed her hips back into the cushions, wriggled her finger inside again, and stepped up the pace, working her pleasure spot until her body was one great raging fire below the waist.

Handle it? Honey, I've already got an ideas board worked up. Maybe a lion skin like Hercules to wear over your shoulders. And young maidens to feed you grapes and rub olive oil into that exquisite body of yours.

Steph's thumb was slipping over every word.

I can see why you've got a bad reputation.

Thank God for predictive text. The base of her hand was hammering against her outer lips, pounding her clit until her whole body sang.

She wondered what Rin was doing right now. Did she have her pants unzipped? Was she naked, even—panting and sighing as she played with herself too? Or was she sitting in some cool rooftop bar, surrounded by musicians and TV stars, calmly sipping a vodka and soda as she teased Steph into madness?

Her next message arrived so fast Steph wondered if she'd been thinking this over in advance.

Or maybe we could go with a wrestling theme? Would you like that? You and some other Amazon tangled up in the sand, naked and oiled up, fighting for glory?

Fuck! Steph groaned out loud. She could picture it, all right—maybe Jill, the short, stocky tough girl on their team, the one with the crew cut, who had to tape over her nipple bars before each game. Steph imagined the two of them puffing and grappling each other for some magazine centrefold, limbs entangling and breasts flattening as they rolled over and over, their fingers clawing into tanned skin. And Rin behind the camera, barking out instructions: *"Grab tighter! Hold her there! That's it, grind that beautiful ass! Jesus, you know what you look like?"*

Steph's orgasm rang in her ears like a goddamned siren. Her muscles were quaking as juices slid down her fingers into the hot, strong palm of her hand.

Weakly, she turned her head to glance at her phone. It had gone quiet again, the screen now a small, black mirror. Then it flashed one more time with a final message from Rin: a single cross. A kiss, maybe, or an *X* to mark the spot.

⟳∽͡ᴐᴄ∽⟲

A month later, an advance copy of the magazine arrived in the mail. As Steph opened the envelope, a letter fell out; it was written in fountain pen on marbled green paper. She hadn't known anyone still sent letters. Was neat handwriting the new punk?

You'll enjoy these, the letter said. (Trust Rin not to bother with question marks or "I hope".) *And thanks. You're a star.*

Steph's fingers itched to flick straight to the pictures, but she wanted to hear from Rin first, from the woman who'd pissed her off, then amazed her, then made her come, all without touching her—except for that one tender brush of her hair.

I'm staying at Women's Life *for now,* Rin wrote. *I figure it's more fun shaking up suburban moms than arguing with twelve-year-old hipster man-babies at the "edgy" publications. And hey, the editor liked your spread. She wants me to do something similar next month with the winner of that fuck-awful reality show* Mile High Club! *See what you've gotten me into?*

Grinning, Steph put down the letter and picked up the magazine. She flicked past famous faces, makeover tips, and psychic advice columns until she saw her own face glowering back at her.

Yes, Rin had kept the dress shots in there. Using some mix of software and imagination, she'd made those original photographs appear to be inside ornate brass frames like something in an art gallery. There was Steph in her blue sparkles, climbing those rickety stairs, looking down in trepidation, slumped miserably against the graffiti-ed wall. But the framed pictures were hung up behind the newer images of Steph pounding away on the treadmill or dribbling the ball expertly between her own legs. The dress pictures became a backdrop to Steph's present-day workout.

Oh, and Rin was good. The pics she'd sent to Steph's phone had been striking enough, but now on a full-sized page, every detail stood out: Steph's smooth, short nails as she grasped the dumbbell, the liquid glinting in the hollow of her throat, and the tension in her body as she held the muddy hem of the blue dress away from her ankles.

One page showed a framed picture of Steph taken through the chain-link fence of the factory yard, tugging glumly at one powder-blue shoulder strap and staring down at her cold, sequined feet. The picture hung on a darkened wall, and beside it, on the door frame, the new Steph was hauling herself into a chin-up. Her back was to the camera, the muscles rolling across her shoulders, her butt high and tight.

Steph traced the page with her fingertips and shook her head. How did Rin do it—see things that other people didn't? And then show them to you so plainly that you couldn't believe you hadn't noticed all along?

And funnily, the dress pictures didn't look so bad. They were grungy and mournful, but not ugly like she'd imagined. And basically harmless, now that they'd been contained in a frame and put in their place.

She turned Rin's letter over.

And, babe, you were right again: my job isn't that important—but neither's yours. Don't make too many more of those sacrifices, okay?

Steph traced one finger over Rin's spidery handwriting. Here was a woman who was not afraid to fail and who made no apologies for who she was. And who could persuade people to see things differently, the way she did. Could Steph do the same?

If you ever feel like giving an interview here at the magazine—something a little more revelatory, yeah? I could swing it with the editor.

A smile played across Steph's lips as she lingered over Rin's final words.

It'd be my absolute fucking pleasure to take your picture again.

Executive Dining

A.L. Brooks

Jamie strutted into the conference room, her gaze taking in the assembled masses in one slow sweep. A good turnout, just as everyone had promised. Most company Christmas parties she'd been to had been dull affairs full of boring speeches. And while there may yet be speeches at this one, the atmosphere she'd walked into was far from dull. It fitted the culture of the company, though. The UK's biggest designer and manufacturer of outdoor kitchens and bars was all about generating a good time. It was cool to see that translated to their in-house events.

To her left, a few people danced near a small sound system that played some of the best cheesy tracks from the eighties and nineties. The stuff her mum liked to listen to. To her right, a huge table of food was laid out, and a number of people piled their plates high. She'd probably hit that next. And throughout the rest of the room and behind her in the corridor were many people drinking from glasses of punch or wine or chugging from bottles of beer.

Yeah, beer—that would be the next stop, then food. She strolled over to the bar area and pulled a longneck out of a bucket of ice. Snapping it open with the opener left on the table next to the bucket, she tilted her head back and took a long drink. Perfect.

As she headed over to the food table, a number of her colleagues and work acquaintances nodded or called a hello.

"Looking good, Jamie!" That came from Ben, her main man in IT.

It always paid to nurture a good relationship with at least one person in IT, and on her first week, six months ago, she and Ben had bonded over Hugo Boss ties. Ben was as serious about his clothes as Jamie and had admired not only what she wore—dark blue suit, crisp white shirt, and yellow tie—but the fact that she dressed true to her butch self. She always had and had ridden the storm of derision through her first two jobs before building up enough of a thick skin not to care anymore.

This was who she was. If people had a problem with it, that was their issue, not hers.

She glanced down at her attire for the party and grinned. Yeah, she was feeling all sorts of good tonight. The grey suit was one she kept for better occasions, but she'd decided to give it an outing tonight. The blue shirt was, for once, left open at the neck—she'd figured it would get too hot at the party to wear a tie. The shoes, though, made the outfit. Italian leather, a darker grey than the suit, with heels that tapped crisply on any hard surface. Lost in here on the carpeted floor of the conference room, but while strolling down the tiled corridor outside, she'd turned heads and caught many an admiring glance from a few men and *lots* of women.

She gulped down another cold mouthful of beer, then smiled. Yeah, she'd been turning female heads since she'd first joined this company, and she liked it. Not that she'd be taking up any of the sly come-ons sent her way here—don't shit where you eat, as her mother always told her. Plus earning toaster ovens was way overrated. She'd had a couple of awkward moments with disgruntled straight women she'd bedded for one night and one night only, once they realised the temporary nature of their assignation.

No, she'd keep her target area to the gay pubs and clubs she visited pretty much every weekend with her group of friends. Sure, even there she might inadvertently hit on a curious straight woman out for a walk on the wild side on a Saturday night, but experience had honed Jamie's discernment of who was likely to give her hassle or not.

She loaded up a plate of food and found a space in the far corner of the room where she could lean against the wall and eat, careful not to spill anything on her suit. She sipped occasionally from her beer, which she propped on a small table beside her. There was a good buzz in the room, and as soon as she'd eaten, she'd probably head over to the dance area and have some fun. She'd just taken the last forkful of food off her plate and lifted it to her mouth when Emily walked into the room. Jamie's heart rate, despite her best intentions, shot up. The fork forgotten where it hung in midair in front of her mouth, she let her gaze track Emily's movement across to the bar via a few waves and hellos, then to the food table. For a moment, Emily disappeared from view, and Jamie snapped back to herself. She darted glances left and right to make sure no one had caught her ogling and crammed the food into her mouth, chewing and swallowing quickly before washing it down with another couple of mouthfuls of beer.

Emily. Shit. She'd forgotten she'd be here.

Emily Dixon was the executive assistant to the CEO. She seemed to be a few years older than Jamie and had been with the company for five years. She knew everything and everyone but was nice about it—no backstabbing stories that did the rounds ever mentioned Emily Dixon.

She was also as hot as hell. The perfect femme, always immaculately turned out with her blonde hair pinned up and wearing classy dresses or skirt suits, her legs wrapped in sheer material that Jamie knew would be incredible to stroke. And the heels. Oh God, the heels. Never less than three inches, usually more like four, lifting Emily's height to match Jamie's, which meant whenever Jamie had to deliver something to the CEO's office and Emily always stood to receive it, Jamie got lost in Emily's sparkling blue eyes.

Emily was the only woman in the company who Jamie would almost forget her mother's words for.

And Emily was *way* out of Jamie's league. By a country mile. Jamie, lowly assistant manager in the post room, who'd dropped out of school at sixteen and bummed one crappy job after another until she'd landed this one, was so not what someone as classy as Emily would go for. Assuming she was even into women. Sure, there'd been that one time she thought she'd caught Emily looking at her with something more than friendliness in her eyes, but it had been so fleeting Jamie had convinced herself she'd imagined it.

"Hey, Jamie, you okay?" Ben appeared by her side.

"What? Oh, yeah, fine. You?"

Ben cocked his head. "You sure? You look a little out of it."

"Ah, just tired. You know how it is." *Don't blush, don't fucking blush.*

He nodded and raised his beer. "Here's to the end of the year. At last!"

They clinked bottles, and Jamie nodded before chugging the last of her beer.

"Get you another?" Ben asked.

"I'll come with you."

Jamie swept up her empty plate and fork and followed Ben across the room to deposit them on the end of the food table. When she turned around to join Ben at the bar, Emily stood in front of her, smiling in a way that made Jamie's bones feel as if they were melting.

"Hi," Emily said.

"Hey. How are you?" She would not make a tit of herself in front of this woman and was pleased her voice came out clear and strong.

"I'm very well. And you?"

Jamie nodded, her confidence coming back, some of her usual swagger seeping into her shoulders, lifting her spine. She could do this. Totally.

"I hate to do this to you at the Christmas party and with everything closing down for the holidays, but there's an issue I need to discuss with you. Do you have a moment?" Emily looked serious, and Jamie tried to beat back the flutterings of panic that launched themselves into full flight in her belly. Had she fucked something up?

"Um, sure." She tried to maintain her cool composure but was not sure she was really pulling it off; a small hint of a smirk played around Emily's lips.

Without another word, Emily strode past Jamie. After only a moment's hesitation, where she flirted with the idea of making Emily turn back to ensure she followed, Jamie decided to play it safe and followed those gorgeous legs out of the room.

They walked down the corridor towards the CEO's office. Both sets of heels clicked in perfect rhythm on the hard floor, and Jamie found the sound strangely soothing. She tried hard not to stare at Emily's ass, which was encased so perfectly in the smooth burgundy material of her skirt, but it was a temptation she failed to resist at least four times before they reached the office.

Emily marched through the door and stood aside to let Jamie pass.

Jamie had only a few seconds to take in her surroundings—opulent furnishings, lush carpet, blinds drawn at all the windows—before the door shut behind her with a loud click and Emily's hand pressed between her shoulder blades.

Taking the hint, Jamie stepped forward towards the large oak desk. It was clear of all the usual things you'd expect to find on an executive's desk; all that remained was a computer monitor and keyboard, offset to the left of the desk as Jamie looked at it. Still totally at a loss to understand what she'd done wrong and why Emily had felt the need to bring her to the CEO's office to tell her, Jamie stopped walking and turned around.

Before she could utter a word, Emily Dixon kissed her. Seriously kissed her and not, it seemed, by accident. Her glossy lips landed on Jamie's with an intent that nearly sent Jamie toppling backwards—only the time she'd spent in the gym strengthening her core held her upright under the onslaught.

And what an onslaught it was. Emily's mouth worked wonders, even more so when Jamie snapped out of her daze and started to kiss Emily back. Their mouths devoured each other, tongues pushing and stroking, their breathing sounding heavy and strained in the quiet of the room. Emily tasted of wine and smelled like peaches. Her hands pushed into Jamie's hair, her fingers clenching the short, black spikes to the point of pain, but Jamie wouldn't have stopped her if she could. It was as if her arms had stopped working—Emily's kisses had all but Jamie's mouth paralysed. Ah, and also her clit, which leapt into action, pulsing between her legs as Emily licked delicately over Jamie's top lip and down over the bottom one. The promise of where else that tongue could lick made Jamie's heart rate spike.

Jamie wasn't used to feeling so out of control in a sexual situation. She was very much a top, and Emily taking over like this was anathema to how Jamie usually enjoyed her sexual encounters. So why couldn't she stop her? Why couldn't she take charge of the situation and show Emily who was really in control?

While a part of her brain screamed, *"Are you fucking crazy? Don't stop this!"* she pulled away, grasping Emily's wrists to ease her hands out of her hair, then using her grip to push Emily a pace backwards.

Emily looked glorious. All mussed up, her tinted lip gloss smeared over and around her lips, her eyes wild and her breathing ragged.

"I... What?" was all Jamie could manage.

Emily laughed. "Don't tell me you haven't thought about doing just that for the last six months." Her voice was low and quiet, the sultriness of her tone sending more delicious throbs through Jamie's clit.

"I...yeah, okay, maybe."

Emily's eyebrows rose. "Maybe?"

Jamie shook her head, trying to clear her thoughts. Even though they weren't kissing, she was still not in control of this situation. That never happened.

"Okay, look, I can admit it. You're hot," Jamie said.

Emily smirked.

"But, um, I don't...I don't get involved with women I work with."

Emily reached out a finger and stroked Jamie's chin. "We don't exactly work together, Jamie. There's no conflict of interest here."

"I know." Jamie almost groaned. Was she completely loopy, standing here turning this down? Emily Dixon wanted her, and she was saying no just because they worked together? She sighed. Yeah, she had to. She'd learned from past experience and from watching the experiences of others that it always ended in tears. Never mind the fact that they were in the CEO's office. Talk about too big a risk for a quick thrill. Even the lovely Emily wasn't worth losing a job over. Jamie took hold of Emily's finger and gently steered it away from her skin. "I'm sorry, it's just something I can't do." She gave Emily's hand a squeeze before letting go.

Emily tilted her head and stared at her for a few seconds. She shrugged. "Okay, my bad. We can just forget this ever happened, okay?"

Jamie nodded dumbly. "Sure."

⚬⚬⚬⚬⚬

Of course, forgetting that Emily Dixon had kissed her face off at the Christmas Party was easier said than done. The good news was, she didn't see Emily that often during her working week. The bad news was that when she did, every memory she had of the way Emily's mouth had reduced her to a whimpering mess came back to haunt her. Emily, of course, seemed entirely unfazed by what they'd had. She was coolness personified and professional to the max—99 percent of the time at least. But every now and then, maybe once in every four or five times they met somewhere in the office, Emily's composure slipped a tad, and her eyes flashed with the desire she'd expressed that night.

And every time they did, Jamie asked herself again why she'd stuck to her guns and turned her away.

Fantasies of Emily were her nighttime guilty pleasure. Over and over again, she played their movie forward from where they'd actually left off to where she imagined they would go, from the kissing to so much more. Her mind ran wild with a variety of scenarios that all had the same outcome: Emily, legs spread wide, flat on her back on the CEO's desk while Jamie slowly fucked her to a blistering orgasm. She'd imagined countless times what Emily's naked body would look like and how she would writhe beneath Jamie's ministrations, how she would beg for more and Jamie would oblige. Of course, she'd also altered the reality a little in her fantasies too—it was Jamie who initiated things, who pushed Emily against the desk and kissed her, Jamie who was in total control of the situation. She couldn't have a good top such as herself looking such a pushover in her own fantasies.

It had been two months since the Christmas party, and winter had kicked in with a vengeance. The doors that opened the delivery bay out to the street had to be left open starting at eight in the morning due to the regularity with which trucks arrived, but that meant that Jamie and her colleagues froze their asses off all day. Jamie found herself volunteering to do more of the actual delivery of items to their recipients as an excuse to get into the warmth of the offices now and again.

She made her way up to the seventh floor, the executive floor, with a cart loaded with portable heaters. Some of the radiators in the main conference rooms were not working as well as they should, and the poor little execs complained of feeling cold in their meetings.

Jamie snorted at the thought, turning her cart out of the goods lift and through the double doors that led to the rooms. As she trundled the cart along the corridor, a familiar voice called out behind her, "Oh, thank God."

She turned slowly, schooling her features so she could pretend the sight of Emily had absolutely no effect on her. Because whatever Emily's choice of outfit for the day, it was sure to set Jamie's libido soaring, and that needed to be stopped in its tracks.

"Those are the heaters, yes?" Emily trotted up alongside Jamie.

"Yep. Four of them, that correct?"

"Perfect." Emily almost purred the word, and for a moment, her gaze wasn't on the cart and its contents but on Jamie herself.

Jamie blinked. "So which rooms do you want them in?"

Emily gave her a smile that said, *"Yes, I was just checking you out again, and yes, we can pretend I wasn't if it makes you feel better."*

Jamie swallowed hard.

"Two each in rooms one and two, please."

"Okay."

Grateful for something to do that took her away from the heat of the moment between them, Jamie pushed the cart another ten metres or so along the corridor and swung it into room one. She hauled two of the large boxes off the cart and followed Emily's pointed finger to place them in two corners.

"Want me to unpack them too?" *Did you really just offer to do that? To stay a little longer in her presence? Good God, what is wrong with you?*

"No, that's okay. I can do that later."

"Cool." Jamie's voice croaked under the pressure of her embarrassment, and she nearly blushed.

Emily smirked but said nothing.

They walked in silence to room two, and Jamie finished unloading the cart.

"Thanks for taking the time to deliver these yourself," Emily said as Jamie wheeled the cart past her and back to the corridor.

"No worries. I just happened to be the next one available when the shipment came in. Could have been any of us, really." *Oh yeah, that sounded so cool. She'll never see through that, you idiot.*

Emily chuckled. "Fair enough." She paused, her gaze unwavering, her tongue slipping shyly from her mouth to wet her lips.

What a total minx. God, why did you turn her down? You could change your mind, of course. She's making it pretty damn clear she hasn't forgotten a thing.

No, too risky! Resist. Resist.

"Right, well. I'll see you around," Jamie said, and before Emily could answer, she swivelled the cart back towards the goods lift.

"Nice to see you, Jamie," Emily said with a laugh in her voice.

⌒∽∂∾⌒

Ten days later, the phone rang in the icy office Jamie shared with her three colleagues.

"Post room, Jamie speaking. How can I help you?"

Emily's smooth tones filled her ears. "Hi, Jamie, this is Emily Dixon."

"Hi." Jamie was glad the office was empty so no one could see her reacting like a damn teenager. It was gone four in the afternoon, and as it was Friday and had been a slow day, she'd sent the rest of her team home for the weekend.

"I'm so glad you're still here," Emily said, talking quickly. "There's something rather urgent that I need your help with."

"Of course. What can I do for you?"

"It would be much easier to explain in person. Could you come up? Meet me at the executive dining room?"

Weird, but okay. "Sure, I'll be there in five."

Jamie checked her tie, adjusted her jacket, then rolled her eyes at herself before hurrying towards the main lifts—no need to take the goods lift and risk sullying her suit when she didn't have to.

Three minutes later, she was at the door to the dining room. It was quiet in the executive suite; she imagined all the execs had already escaped for the weekend. There was no sign of Emily, but the door was slightly ajar, and she could hear movement from within. She took a deep breath, told herself to stay cool, and knocked on the door.

"Come in!" Emily said.

Jamie pushed open the door and stepped into the room. It was dimly lit, only some lights on the side walls casting their golden glow towards the ceiling. Emily was at the end of the room farthest from Jamie, tidying away some plates.

She didn't turn from her task. "Shut the door."

Also weird, but whatever. Jamie shut the door behind her.

"Be a good girl and lock it too, would you?"

Jamie had turned, and her hand was halfway towards the lock before her brain kicked in. "Er, what?"

Emily's chuckle was throaty. "Lock the door, Jamie."

Her clit really shouldn't be throbbing. Not so quickly and at such innocuous words.

But it was.

Hard.

She did as she was told and flipped the lock. Her hands shook, and she flexed them a couple of times to try to ease the trembling. It made no difference.

She turned slowly back to the room. Emily now stood at the end of the huge mahogany dining table, the end where there were no chairs, the area left free for access to the cupboards containing all the dining accoutrements. She smiled at Jamie.

"Very good." Her gaze flitted up and down Jamie's body.

Jamie gulped.

"Why don't you come over here so I can tell you what all of this is about?" Emily beckoned slightly with one hand. It was as if she'd used some kind of force field to propel Jamie forward. Her feet moved of their own accord without any conscious input from her brain. Seconds later, she stood in front of Emily, trying hard not to fall into those piercing blue eyes.

"So." Emily took one step forward into Jamie's personal space, laying a finger on the lapel of Jamie's jacket and stroking the fabric.

Jamie's heart thudded.

"I have some news."

"Y-yes?" *Oh, for fuck's sake, get a grip! Come on, snap out of it!* But she couldn't. Emily had her under a spell she couldn't fight. Didn't want to.

"Yes," Emily said, her breath warm against Jamie's face. "You see, today is my last day here. I have a new job."

"You...you do?"

Emily nodded. The finger stroking Jamie's lapel snuck lower to the single button that held the jacket closed. A second later and the button had been snapped open. The two halves of the jacket fell to the side, revealing more of the burgundy shirt Jamie had paired with the black suit that morning.

"I do. After five years, it was time for a new challenge, a bigger company. Besides, continuing to work here was preventing me from...pursuing...other interests." She sighed sweetly as her hands pushed Jamie's jacket open still farther. "So you know what that means, don't you?"

Jamie had absolutely no idea—her brain was in meltdown, her entire being focussed on where Emily's hand would go next. She watched, her mouth slightly agape, her breathing heavy, as Emily ran her hand behind the silk of Jamie's tie, the backs of her fingers trailing a path up between Jamie's breasts.

"It means," Emily said, "that after today, Jamie, we will no longer work for the same company. So if we decided to do something about this undeniable attraction between us, we wouldn't be breaking your commendable, albeit rather silly, rule about not getting involved with someone you work with."

Jamie blinked rapidly. Holy shit, Emily was right! *Hang on, she made me lock the door. Does that mean…? Oh. My. God.*

"Jamie," Emily said, her tone firm, forcing Jamie to raise her eyes and look straight at her.

"Yes?"

"Kiss me."

No hesitation, no questions. Jamie lunged forward, her hands reaching for Emily's hips to yank her tight against her body as her lips pressed against Emily's soft, wet mouth. The kiss was fierce, searing Jamie's body with heat. Emily was all softness and warmth, melding herself to Jamie with a soft groan, her hands once again landing in Jamie's hair and tugging sharply. Emily's breasts mushed against hers, and Jamie's hands drifted to cup Emily's beautifully round ass and pull her even closer. She felt something under the material of Emily's skirt, something that felt very much like the straps of a suspender belt, and she groaned at the thought of it.

Emily grabbed her hands and moved them away from her ass, bringing them up to her waist instead. Okay, so she wanted to go a little slower. Jamie could do that. After all, just kissing Emily was pretty damn hot, and it was even more exciting knowing that now, at last, she could let her desire for this sexy woman have full rein. So she'd let them kiss for a little longer, keep Emily happy, then she'd—

Emily pulled back, a wicked smile on her face. "Very good," she said, as if grading homework. "But I can't have you getting too carried away just yet."

Huh? Jamie was in a daze. The kiss had scrambled her brain and drenched her underwear. Her limbs felt like jelly. But even so, she shouldn't be standing here feeling as if she were in front of a teacher waiting for her next assignment. *Come on, get back in the game—get her naked!*

She reached for Emily, but she lightly sidestepped away, a gentle laugh escaping her.

"No, Jamie. That's not how this is going to go." She stared at Jamie, biting her bottom lip in a way that made Jamie's pussy ache. "First, you'll take your jacket off. Please."

Jamie stared at her. *Hm. Well, okay, taking a jacket off is cool. Maybe she wants us to go one piece at a time, alternating. Yeah, okay, I'll let her have her little game.* She shucked out of the jacket and tossed it over the back of the nearest chair, then waited for Emily to remove something—perhaps her shirt, because God knows it would be awesome to see what she had to offer beneath that.

Emily, however, didn't move. Still with that saucy smile on her face, she motioned towards Jamie's torso. "Shirt and tie next. Please."

No. No way. There had to be some give and take, didn't there? *I mean, just because I'm not entirely in control of this like I want to be, she has to play fair, doesn't she?*

Emily tilted her head. "Problem?"

"How come I'm the only one undressing?" Jamie's tone was bordering on sullen. Once again, she was back to acting like a teenager. How the hell did Emily do that to her?

Emily stepped forward until she was mere inches away. "Jamie, you are one gorgeous butch of a woman, but you still haven't figured this out yet, have you?"

When Jamie said nothing—because she couldn't lie and say she had *any* of this figured out—Emily continued.

"Honey, I'm as top as it gets. If you want any piece of this"—she gestured at her own body—"you're going to have to work hard to get it." She leaned in and placed a soft kiss on Jamie's mouth. "But trust me, it'll be so worth it."

Jamie's entire pussy throbbed. Air seemed hard to come by, and words were a fragment of memory from a life before this moment in this room. Everything was upside down. She was about to be topped, for the first time in her life. She should be fighting it. But God help her, she couldn't muster any enthusiasm for trying to turn this tide.

She nodded.

Emily's smile returned as she stepped back. "Good girl."

Hands shaking, Jamie undid her tie and threw it behind her. The shirt was next, as instructed, also tossed carelessly away. Emily didn't have to speak this time—she merely pointed at the trousers. Jamie kicked off her shoes, yanked off her socks, and had the trousers undone and off and thrown behind her in record time.

A vague corner of her brain registered that she was now standing in her sports bra and boxers in the executive dining room late on a Friday afternoon—not something she would ever have envisaged in her future when she first took this job. *Amazing where your career can take you*, she thought, then decided thinking was overrated and instead focussed on the arousal that coursed through her veins as Emily's gaze raked over her body. Jamie was a gym addict. Her body, while not slim, was toned in all the right places. Emily seemed pleased with what she could see; her eyes narrowed slightly, and despite her controlled demeanour, the slightest hint of pink tinged her cheeks.

"Arms up." She stepped back into Jamie's space.

Jamie obeyed and gasped as Emily's somewhat cool fingers gripped the bottom band of the bra and pulled. She wasn't delicate about it, and the frisson of pain as the bra dragged over her nipples had Jamie moaning and closing her eyes.

"Keep your arms up."

Jamie opened her eyes again. Emily stared at her nipples, which were solid nubs in the midst of her puckered flesh. She had goose bumps all over her skin, but it wasn't from the cold.

Emily moved again, this time slipping her cool hands into the back of Jamie's boxers. Always one of her greater erogenous zones, her buttocks tingled with sensation as Emily slowly worked the boxers down. Jamie almost whimpered with sorrow when Emily's hands left her ass to tug at the side of the boxers. But then they were down, and she was kicking them away, and her pussy, open to the air, cried out for Emily's cool fingers to find it.

"Open your legs."

How could three little words cause her to gush so much fluid from her pussy? She parted her thighs, her feet now wide apart.

"Very nice." Emily nodded. "So nice to see a full covering of hair too."

Her fingers, without warning, trailed through Jamie's full bush, stopping just shy of Jamie's swollen clit. Jamie arched into the touch with a long groan.

"Oh, someone's ready, aren't they?"

"Shit, I've been ready since Christmas." Jamie gasped as Emily tugged on her crisp hairs, and Emily's laughter rang out.

"I knew it," Emily whispered, close to Jamie's ear, her breath making Jamie shiver. "Now, on your back, please." She pointed at the table.

"Are you ser—?" The look Emily gave her cut her off.

Holy shit.

The table's height made it easy for Jamie to perch her ass on the edge and lie back. It wasn't that comfortable, but there was no way she was going to waste breath pointing that out now.

Emily's hands grabbed her knees and pulled her legs wide open. Jamie planted her feet on the edge of the table, her knees bent, and gazed along the length of her own body to the fully clothed woman standing between her open legs.

"Arms above your head." Emily's voice was firm, but there was an edge there now. Just a slight huskiness that hinted at what the sight of Jamie, spread out before her, was doing to her. The flush of pride that shot through Jamie surprised her, but she accepted it as her due.

She stretched her arms upwards, her breasts lifting as she did so. Her nipples were so hard with the anticipation of what Emily might do to her in this position, they were almost painful. Never mind what it was doing to her poor, desperate pussy. She was in uncharted territory now. Usually, by the time she got this naked, her new lover had already had a couple of orgasms and was only too eager to give back to Jamie whatever she needed. She hadn't even seen Emily's tits yet, for crying out loud. Laughter threatened to bubble up from deep in her chest, but she bit it back.

Neither the time nor place, Jamie.

Emily trailed a finger from Jamie's knee down her thigh, stopping just short of her aching pussy.

"Emily," Jamie breathed, knowing it was probably a mistake but unable to help herself. She needed something from Emily and soon. The waiting was unbearable.

Emily chuckled and repeated the slow stroke down the other leg from the same starting point to the same torturous end point. Then she bent forward and trailed her tongue from Jamie's entrance to her clit—just the tip of it, Jamie thought, as the touch was so delicate. Jamie twitched and moaned and silently begged for more.

"Mmm, what a perfect dish for eating at such a fine table." Emily licked again, the same pathway, the same briefest amount of pressure. "I've been fantasising about eating you here for quite a while now."

She licked again, a little harder.

Jamie's hips moved upwards of their own volition.

"Tut, tut." Emily stepped back. "Impatient little madam, aren't you?"

"You're killing me." Jamie stared at Emily. "You've got me where you want me, haven't you? Come on. Please." She'd given in, and that was okay. She could live with that, given it was this incredible woman she'd given in to. Begging out loud might be a step too far, but she bordered on not caring about that either.

"Hm," Emily said. "I don't have you *quite* where I want you. But…"

She turned away, and Jamie lifted her head to watch where she went. Why was she walking away? Emily reached for a bag on top of one of the cupboards. It looked as if it was made of velvet in a deep red colour.

When Jamie saw what Emily pulled from the bag, her eyes widened.

"Now," Emily said, turning back to Jamie. "You only have to say the word and this goes back in the bag. But this"—she stepped closer until her thighs were pressed between Jamie's—"is exactly how I want you."

Jamie swallowed. Stared at the dildo in Emily's hand. It wasn't huge, thank God. Oh sure, Jamie had tried it once on herself to see what it was like. The feeling of being filled had been good, and she'd made herself come by stroking her clit as she slowly fucked her own pussy. She just couldn't ever imagine letting her lovers do it to her the way she did to them. To lie down and let them push inside her, let them fuck her, let them thrust in and out, in and…

Her pussy clenched as the image of Emily doing just that in the next few minutes sent a bolt of arousal so fierce through her, she nearly cried out.

How was this possible? How did Emily make this happen? How did Jamie let it? But, oh fuck, she wanted it. *Bad.*

She kept her mouth shut, and Emily's look was a mix of triumphant and tender.

Emily leaned over Jamie to set the dildo on the table, a condom and a sachet of lube next to it. Jamie blinked and swallowed, trying to get her breathing under control, but the thought of what Emily was about to do to her made that one of the most difficult things she'd ever attempted.

When she straightened, Emily let her hands slide down the length of her skirt to its hem, and as she pulled it up, Jamie saw that it wasn't stockings that covered Emily's gorgeous legs—it was hold-ups. It wasn't a suspender belt around her waist—it was a harness. Red leather matching the red of the dildo and snug against Emily's pale hips. Emily wore no underwear, and Jamie saw dark curls between her legs, both they and the harness doing too good a job of hiding the treasure that lay underneath. But Emily was wet, Jamie could tell that much, and that sense of pride puffed out her chest again. *She'd* done that. She'd made Emily Dixon wet.

She wanted to find words to tell Emily how hot she looked, how she couldn't wait for Emily to strap that thing on and get it inside her, but her mouth had gone dry and her voice had deserted her. She watched, entranced, as Emily tucked her skirt into its own waistband, then reached again for the dildo. She sucked her tummy in to give herself enough room to force the dildo between her skin and the harness, then it was in and through the O-ring, sitting proud and ready. It took Emily no time to roll the condom on and lube up, and Jamie knew, in that moment, that Emily had done this many times before.

A streak of jealousy heated her skin, and she laughed inwardly. Crazy.

Then the only thoughts whirling through her brain were those of pleasure and need and lust as Emily pressed against the edge of the table with her thighs and placed the head of the dildo against Jamie's pussy. She rubbed it up and down the length of Jamie, the lube cool against Jamie's lips, the teasing nature of the touch causing her to pant and gasp.

"Jamie." Emily's voice seemed loud in the small space between them.

Jamie forced her eyes up to meet Emily's heated gaze.

"Now I have you *exactly* where I want you." Emily's voice was ragged despite her apparent composure.

She pushed inside Jamie—slow, so slow it was as if the pleasure from it might undo Jamie, tear her apart, unmake her. Then Emily was deep, as deep as she could get, and the thrusting started, and Jamie suddenly knew. Knew what all her previous partners had groaned and cried and shouted about because, holy hell, this was exquisite. The dildo was ribbed, as was the condom, and while those sensations were entirely new and something Jamie knew she'd want to feel again and again, she knew, deep down, it was the surrender that turned her on the most. Being at Emily's mercy, doing Emily's bidding, being her good girl—this was what had Jamie's mind reeling and her arousal blazing an uncharted trail across her whole body.

As she thrust, Emily reached for Jamie's breasts and tweaked and pulled at her nipples. It was torture. No, it was paradise. Oh God, it was both. Emily's hips worked harder, driving deeper. Jamie helped her by opening her legs farther, lifting her feet to hook them behind Emily's ass and pull her in.

It was wanton.

Totally bottom.

Perfect.

"Good girl," Emily whispered. She leaned forward, driving even deeper, and kissed Jamie, her tongue lazy in and around Jamie's mouth.

Jamie groaned and moaned and made sounds she didn't even have a name for. Like a good girl, she kept her arms above her head and let Emily do what she wanted, but God, how she wished she could hold her, bring her even closer. Maybe next time, if she was a good girl…

Beads of sweat formed on Emily's forehead. She was really working Jamie, fucking her faster, her hands now planted on the table on either side of Jamie's head, her lustrous blonde hair escaping its ties and wild strands framing her damp face.

Jamie's orgasm built. It shocked her, having never known she could come from penetration alone, but there was something about the motion, about the way part of the harness pressed against her tormented clit that meant she was close. So close.

"I… God!" Jamie gulped in air. "I'm going to—"

"Yes," Emily hissed. "*Yes*."

And Jamie did, howling out her pleasure in an extended cry as white-hot ribbons of climax rippled over every inch of her skin. She threw her head back, her legs jerking, which only extended her pleasure as each twitch brought Emily and her dildo into closer contact with Jamie's swollen clit. Emily still pumped, not as deep, but keeping up her motion, and it kept Jamie's pleasure flowing through her, down her legs, down her arms to her fingers, which tingled with the sensations.

Emily stopped eventually, running a hand over her brow, pushing away those errant strands of hair, but still she remained inside Jamie, and Jamie had no complaints. It was, she knew, exactly where Emily should be.

Jamie closed her eyes, her breathing slowing. Emily's lips on hers, soft and tender, had her opening her eyes again. Emily watched her, an enigmatic smile on her face.

Oh shit, how long had her eyes been closed? Surely Emily must need some attention. *Shit, how could I forget that?*

"Sorry, just give me a minute, and I'll take care of you."

She attempted to move, to sit up, but Emily pushed her back down. "We can deal with that later." She eased out of Jamie.

It was a little sore, but Jamie wasn't about to complain. Emily stood before her, her face shining, her eyes bright, the dildo glistening between her legs. Fucking glorious.

"Later?" Did Emily mean…?

"Well, do you have any plans for tonight?"

Exultant, Jamie shook her head. Well, she had sort of said she might go to the pub with her usual gang, but fuck that.

She still hadn't seen Emily's tits, after all.

58 Seconds

Harper Bliss

I see her every morning, along with hundreds of other commuters. I start my journey at Holborn tube station, and, as far as I can tell, hers ends there. Unless she takes a bus elsewhere. I don't know, but I've made up many stories in my head. If she gets off at Holborn, she must work there. But we only cross each other on the extra-long escalator transporting me deep underground in the morning. I go down; she goes up.

This being London, I can't rely on the punctuality of public transport to see her every morning, so there's that added tension. Because of this, I've perfected my timing for maximum exposure to Hot Blonde, as I like to call her.

I stand in front of my front door at precisely eight o'clock. It takes me exactly six minutes and forty-three seconds to reach the barrier where I tap in with my Oyster card. This being peak rush hour, I always have to queue between thirty and forty seconds, then take a few more steps, and I'm on my way down.

The escalator is long, and it takes fifty-eight seconds for it to carry me all the way down if I stand still and don't rush down the steps. Fifty-eight seconds of exhilaration and anticipation. Sometimes we cross each other just as I've stepped on, and she's gone in a flash, no matter how much I crane my neck. Other times, I can see her riding up, and I can revel in the moment. I can luxuriate in the riveting anticipation of our gazes locking for an instant. Her eyes are light, although I can't see their exact colour. The distance between the escalator going down and the one going up is too big.

Sometimes, when I haven't spotted her, I linger in the short corridor where incoming and outgoing foot traffic meet. How can I start my day without seeing her? I can, of course, but it's nowhere near as fun. As a result, I spend my day thinking about her even more.

On more than one occasion, I've fantasised that the reason I didn't see her on the escalator that morning is because she's waiting for me to exit at my destination in Shoreditch Station. Then she follows me stealthily, finds out I work in an art gallery, and strolls in. This fantasy has a few obvious flaws, chief among them that we've never exchanged more than a glance and that she probably isn't as crazy as I am. She looks very together. Long escalators like that provide an excellent people watching opportunity, but no one has ever stuck out at me the way she does.

She's tall and has short blonde hair, the aforementioned light eyes, and even though she doesn't smile—not many people do on their daily commute—there's something very inviting about her face. It's one of those captivating faces you can't help looking at. I have examined the people behind me on the escalator, but hardly anyone ever looks up from their phone when they cross Hot Blonde.

Maybe it's just me, then.

What I have noticed, however, is that she always looks back. Every morning, we exchange a glance. As I glide down and she floats up, in that second our paths cross, we look into each other's eyes. That must mean something. You don't cut your gaze to a stranger every morning for no reason. Maybe she sees in me what I see in her. Maybe we have that secret lesbian thing going. What's it called for lesbians? Dykedar? That elusive gut instinct that makes you look twice.

Or maybe she recognises me from somewhere. Maybe she's been to the gallery before.

The first time our gazes lingered, I couldn't look away. I craned my neck as far as it would go, earning an accusatory glance from the passenger behind me—because how dare I deviate from escalator etiquette? But it was as though my glance was glued to her, and I had to really force myself to turn my head, look in front of me, and make sure I didn't stumble off the last step once it disappeared into the floor.

She was there again the next morning and the morning after that. Then it was the weekend, and whereas I have to work on Saturdays, she obviously doesn't. It's also much harder to time things on a Saturday because the flow of commuters is much lighter and the escalator isn't as packed.

This has been going on for five weeks. The past few Mondays, I've lain in my bed, awake at my usual time, even though it's my day off, pondering whether I should get up and go through my usual routine just to see her. But that's ridiculous. And I wouldn't be taking advantage of my freedom. Which I plan to do today. I'm going to turn my fantasy on its head. I'm going to wait for her at the exit of Holborn Station, obscured by the mass of people, and discreetly follow her to see where she works.

I've been ready to go for half an hour, but I have to bide my time. I've calculated and recalculated, and if I leave in a few minutes and position myself at the stakeout spot I've decided on—maximum view, minimum chance of getting funny looks—I can't miss her, provided she's on schedule and all the other parameters work in my favour.

Of the five weeks I've been seeing her, at nine minutes past eight in the morning, she's missed four days. An astoundingly small number. It can't be a coincidence, or so I tell myself as I check my appearance in the mirror again. I push my thick-rimmed glasses up the bridge of my nose. I straighten my blazer. I practice my smile. I try to breathe through the nerves that soar in my belly.

"Am I crazy for doing this?" *A little*. It's a leap of faith. Five weeks of escalator foreplay is long enough. What will happen if I don't do this? We'll keep making eyes at each other every morning? Maybe that's how she wants it. Maybe I'm just a distraction from the daily grind. Maybe she has a wife at home. Or a husband. I don't know anything, and it's what excites me the most. She's a blank canvas for me to project onto everything I want in a woman. A beautiful, blonde-haired canvas, but a blank one nonetheless.

Then it's time to put my dykedar, my gut instinct, and my projections to the test. One last breath and I'm out the door.

There's a wobble in my step, but I tell myself I'm just observing. She must have noticed by now that I don't commute on Mondays if, indeed, she has noticed me at all. I try to enjoy the fresh air but end up inhaling rancid exhaust fumes. My senses seem more aware: my sense of smell is keener, my eyes skitter from here to there, and I don't wear the noise-cancelling headphones that make commuting bearable. I don't want to miss anything. I need to be alert.

I have no exact plan, nothing I can put into words that I want to get out of this. I just want to have tried. I want to have made a move because who knows? Maybe she's the one. Stranger things have happened.

I scold myself for thinking like this. Perhaps I've been alone for too long, haven't been touched in too long. The other day, on my way to work, I listened to a podcast in which a professor of psychology claimed that human beings can die from a lack of being touched.

In the distance, I can see the sign for the tube—the familiar red circle with the blue line going across. The entrance is mobbed as usual. It won't be a problem at all to blend in. The only problem I envision is spotting her in the crowd. But I have to trust my instinct, my powers of perception, and perhaps rely on serendipity a fraction. Something inside me knows that I won't be able to miss her. That if she's there at the planned time, I will see her. Because that's how it's meant to be. If not, then we'll forever be two faces in the crowd. Two strangers passing on the escalator.

To look less conspicuous while lingering outside the tube station, I buy a cup of coffee from the Dunkin' Donuts next to it. I lean against a lamppost. I'm in the way, but the pavement is so narrow here and the crowd too vast for me to stand anywhere else and still have a good view of the people being spewed from the tube.

I thought about waiting inside but considered it too risky. Nobody lingers inside a tube station at this hour, not even tourists. Everyone gets swept up in the perpetual motion of commuters—there's no escape.

I sip from my Americano while I keep my gaze glued to the mouth of the tube station. It's all about patience now and not averting my gaze. I have no idea which way she will go once she's out.

Seconds tick by as though they're minutes. I figure only about five minutes must have passed, although it feels more like five hours. Nerves coil into a tight knot in my stomach. Time passes, and she still hasn't shown up. I'm beginning to think I've missed her. My plan might be solid, but it's not fail-safe. And I do wear glasses. My vision could be the one thing letting me down, and it's not something my enthusiasm or eagerness can overcome. I can't see better just because I want to see her.

Then, like the very picture from my dreams, there she is. She's coming at me fast, but her gaze is aimed straight ahead, while I stand on the side of the pavement. I've never seen her so close before. She's wearing a pristine white shirt underneath a navy blazer. She wears a variation on this every day, making me suspect she's a consultant or something of the sort. It's their uniform. But, again, I can only speculate.

She's only a few yards away from me. I inhale deeply, hoping to catch some of her scent, but I only smell coffee and pollution. I don't move, because I don't want to draw attention to myself as she scoots past me. There are at least two rows of people between us, and she'd have to look to her left—with intent—to see me. She heads to the pedestrian crossing and waits. I swivel around and prepare to move. I need to cross when the light goes green next at the same time she does; otherwise, I risk losing her. Not an option now that I have her in my sight.

She doesn't check her phone, nor does she look to her left and right to spot for any openings in traffic before the light turns green. She waits patiently, unlike most of the other people around her. I like that about her. She doesn't feel the need to defy the rules to gain a few insignificant seconds. She doesn't put her own benefit above traffic laws. I don't know why, but it pleases me. Or maybe I'm happy that I don't need to follow her as she makes her way through moving traffic. High Holborn on a Monday morning is no walk in the park.

The traffic light turns green, and the pedestrians start crossing. I follow, my gaze trained on her. She takes the road ahead in the direction of my flat, but whereas I would turn left at the next street to go home, Hot Blonde walks straight ahead. Now that we're on street level together, I can see she's taller than me, and I need to ramp up my pace to keep up with her. There are about five people walking in between us at various speeds. She reaches the next crossing. The light is green, so she keeps walking. When I reach the same crossing, the light flashes to red, and I have to make a split-second decision. If I wait, I will lose her. So I dash across the street as quickly as I can. I'm not the only one. Hot Blonde is unaware of the goings-on—and the traffic infractions—behind her. I take a few deep breaths and follow her again. She doesn't wear headphones, also an oddity for a London commuter. How does she shut out all the noise? Maybe she doesn't need to. Maybe she's naturally zen. In my head, she's so many things. All things she's probably not. She rounds the next corner. She slows her pace a little. There are three high-rises next to each other. My guess is she'll be heading inside one of them. Which one will it be?

She runs a hand through her short hair and disappears into the doorway of the first building. A pang of something—disappointment because she's out of sight?—rips through me. I halt in front of the building. The sliding doors close in front of me, and I can't look in, because they're made out of frosted glass. I look at the nameplates to the right of the door. There are about a dozen, all of them company names. She could work for any of these firms. And I'm none the wiser. Deflation courses through me. The rush of excitement I felt while I was on her tail disappears, the sudden lack of adrenalin leaving me empty—and empty-handed at that. What's my next move?

I glance around. There's a Costa Coffee across the road. I go there often enough, and I proclaim it my lunchtime stakeout place. Hot Blonde is not getting away from me. I still have a chance. If she goes out for lunch—maybe even to Costa?—I can follow her again. There are a lot of ifs and whens about my plan, but I still feel as though I have luck on my side. I still have a chance, although I'm not sure of what exactly I have a chance at. I head home to gather my wits and prepare for my lunchtime pursuit.

I'm at Costa Coffee at eleven. No seats are available by the window, and it's too cold to sit outside. I wait until one of the high stools frees up, then stake my claim. I nurse my second Americano of the day. I'll need to switch to decaf soon. I brought a book to fake-read while I keep my gaze on Hot Blonde's building. What has she been working on? Was I wise to leave the entrance unguarded for a few hours? She could have gone out for a meeting. So much could have happened. This entire day is a long shot. And all of this because of a woman on the escalator. I must have truly lost my mind, but if I have, I've lost it to her.

Time passes slowly, but it does pass. It always does. I've bought a second coffee—decaf this time—when, around noon, a few people trickle out of the building, looking for lunch. I guzzle my coffee in case I need to hurry out of the door. There's a road between my vantage point and the entrance, and there's a good amount of traffic. But I'm still confident I can spot Hot Blonde anywhere.

The sight reminds me of this morning at the tube station. More and more people flood out of the building. I sit up a bit straighter to enhance my view. No sign of her. Maybe she doesn't eat lunch, or maybe she's one of those busy types who claims she doesn't have time for it and quickly spoons up some yoghurt in front of her always-flickering computer screen.

My heart skips a beat. I nearly drop the cup of coffee from my trembling hands. I must have lost focus for a few seconds because Hot Blonde is only a few steps away from the window I'm sitting at—as though I'm on display. She's coming this way. She halts at the window. She peers inside, probably sizing up the queue, then her gaze descends, and she looks straight at me.

I'm face-to-face with Hot Blonde. This is the closest we've been. Something shifts inside me, as though every fibre in my body knows this is my moment and every one of my cells needs to work to make this happen for me. I smile. I need to spark recognition in her. For a fraction of a second, I fear she may have no clue who I am, that she's been looking straight through me all these weeks, but then her lips curve into a smile, and her face that was already so inviting, so captivating, turns into a display of warmth and openness and, yes, recognition.

I slip off my stool and hurry outside. This is it. This is the moment I've been waiting for. It can either be a disappointment or the best thing that has ever happened to me.

"Hi." I stand a few feet from her. On the street, cyclists and taxis hurtle past us; hungry office workers are hunting for food. "I'm Janet. I…" What to say? *Come on, Janet. You've prepared for this moment.*

Hot Blonde stretches out her arm toward me. "Sharon. Nice to meet you." *Sharon.* Her voice is low and brimming with the sort of confidence I could do with right about now.

"And you." I take her hand in mine. I'm touching Hot Blonde. This is too easy. Or maybe it wasn't all in my head. This is me meeting Sharon. This is the beginning of something.

"I've imagined this moment many a time. And here we are." Slowly, Sharon withdraws her hand.

"Would you like to get some lunch?" There's no chance I can swallow even the tiniest bite of food.

"Sure. I was just about to head in here." She nods at Costa. "It seems quite packed, though."

"D'you know what? I live just around the corner, and I'm sure I can rustle us up something."

"Are you inviting me to your place?" Sharon's full-wattage smile is almost too much for me. As though she knows, she throws in a chuckle.

I grin. "Too forward?"

"What's too forward, really?" She cocks her head. "I happen to be rather fond of forward people. Lead the way."

"Gladly." Her words have given me confidence—have given me wings, really. We fall into step and head towards my flat in silence.

I live on the first floor, so I guide us up the stairs. Usually, climbing one flight of stairs doesn't leave me this out of breath, but I'm panting when I unlock the door. I invite Sharon in, and then we stand in my living room.

"Let me see what I have in the fridge," I say.

"I'm not that hungry." Sharon takes a step closer. "Well, I *am* but not for food." She shoots me another of her bright smiles. I hardly know what to do with it. I gaze into her eyes and determine their colour once and for all. They're blue. I have a blue-eyed blonde in my home who's hungry but not for food. I know exactly how she feels.

"What might you be hungry for?"

"The woman who's been eyeing me on the Holborn subway escalator for the past five weeks. I'm utterly ravenous for her." She inclines her head and locks her gaze with mine.

I suck my bottom lip into my mouth. I'm not sure yet how to handle my dream coming true. "Ditto." I want to ask how much time she has, but I'm afraid it will break the fragile magic between us.

She glances around the flat. "Nice place." Her eyes linger at a row of picture frames to our left. Her lips curve up again. "You have exquisite taste." She steps closer and curls her fingers around my wrists. I can smell her perfume now. Her hot scent. Her desire for me. It's all on display; it crackles in the air. Her fingers tighten. My pulse picks up speed underneath them. I couldn't have dreamed it any better. Sharon is doing exactly what I want her to do. She's taking charge. With my wrists in her grip, she backs me up against the wall.

She gazes down at me, then brings her lips to my ear. "I think this is where I'll have you." It sounds more like a threat than a promise. My blood pounds in my veins. My heart's all the way in my throat. All I want is for her to have me here, against this wall.

She doesn't ask if that's all right with me. I'm guessing she can see it in my glance. She can easily read it from my body language, from the way I'm surrendering to her.

She presses her body against mine. Her fingers remain wrapped around my wrists. She brings her lips a fraction away from mine. I can feel her breath on me, smell her perfume from up close—it's light and fruity and intoxicating. She stares into my eyes as though she knows exactly what I want. But then she surprises me again by releasing one of my wrists and bringing her hand to my cheek. With the back of her fingers, she caresses me.

"What would you like me to do to you?"

Her fingers have reached my lips. I'm not sure if I should answer; I'm not sure I can, with one of her fingers now skating along my bottom lip. Her touch is electrifying. It spreads to every cell of my body. My clit stands to attention, the once familiar tingle in my belly. The start-up sign, as I used to call it back in the day when I was still touched like this regularly. My engine of lust revs.

"Hmm?" Sharon plants the lightest of kisses next to my mouth. Another electrifying touch.

"Kiss me properly."

A small smile breaks on her face. My voice sounds strong, as though I know what I want and am not mortified to express it.

She releases my other wrist and brings both her hands to my chin, cupping my jaw. Before her lips land on mine, she inhales deeply, then she finally kisses me. Her lips are soft and somehow familiar. When she opens her mouth, mine opens with hers. Our tongues dance, and it's the most exquisite sensation. I have to keep my knees from buckling.

I wrap my arms around her neck and draw her close. Her breasts push against mine. I can make out the contours of her body, the hardness in some places and the delicious softness in others.

We can't seem to break from our kiss. It goes on and on, turning my legs more to jelly with every second it progresses. Sharon is the world's best kisser, or at least the best kisser that has ever planted her lips on mine. Her tongue swirls in my mouth, so soft yet so confident. As though our mouths were only ever meant to kiss one another.

Then she pulls back. When she looks at me, I see the storm gathering in her eyes. The kiss has undone her as much as it has me. We're on an even keel again. I can feel it. The energy between us is different. I bet that, if I wanted to, I could turn the tables on Sharon and press her against the wall. But that's not what I want.

Sharon plants her hands next to my head, as though she needs to steady herself. Maybe she does.

"What would you like me to do next, Janet?" The way she says my name triggers something in me, revs up my engine again, and keeps it humming at an accelerating pace.

I narrow my eyes. "Fuck me."

Another one of her small smiles. The bright, wide one she greeted me with seems to have been relegated to another lifetime, to before she pushed me against the wall. Even though she doesn't say anything, I read it as a resounding yes. She runs a finger along my cheek again slowly, like villains in movies run a knife along their victims' necks before cutting their throats.

My breath becomes shallower. My nipples press against my bra. I want Sharon so much; it's becoming more like an ache. Like a void in me that can only be filled with her fingers.

Her gaze remains on me. She looks steady, while I'm falling apart. Her finger glides across my throat to my collarbone, dips into my blouse.

It travels up again, but it's only a diversion because it heads straight back down, touching me, light as a feather, and circles one of my nipples. My nipple is so hard it's visible through the fabric of my bra and blouse. It screams out my desire.

Sharon is playing me as if she has never done anything else in her life, and it lights a fire in me that's been dormant for too long. Her finger doesn't travel to my other breast, but she undoes the first button of my blouse. I guess the act of slipping the buttons from their holes is too arduous a task for her flaring desire as well because next thing I know, she rips at my blouse, pulling the buttons loose in one go and displaying my bra-clad breasts.

A gasp escapes me. Her sudden aggression excites me. The promise of it is almost too much. She regards my chest. The grin on her lips tells me she likes what she sees. All of this and I've barely touched her. Maybe she's getting her kicks out of doing this to me—it sure looks like it.

She comes for my breasts next. She cups them with her hands, but only ever so briefly, before pulling my bra down and freeing my nipples. They reach up, aching for her touch. She runs the pad of her finger over the right one, with that featherlight touch again, only to give my nipple a vicious but delicious pinch a second after.

"Aah."

It spurs her on. She tweaks my nipple—pinch and release, pinch and release—while her lips find my neck, and she kisses me there, lighting up all the parts of me that were still waiting to catch fire.

"Oh, God." I twirl my fingers around her short blonde hair. "Oh, Sharon." I say her name as though any other names are meaningless to me from now on.

This makes her look up and withdraw her divine lips from my neck. She glances at me, and I know what's in her glance. I can read her the way she reads me, the way she's been reading my body with her fingers. *Are you ready?* her eyes ask. I nod. I've been ready for the past five weeks.

She doesn't tear the button off my trousers but flips it open reverently, as though the act of it is an important moment in our short history together. It is. My body heats up with the anticipation of where her hand is headed. Those fingers inside me. Just the thought of it is enough for another round of violent pulsing in my clit. She unzips me. I help her push my trousers down. I've waited five weeks for this. Any extra second now is pure agony.

I heel off my shoes and step out of my trousers, a little miffed that I'm still wearing my knickers, but Sharon's in charge. She remains crouched, her head level with my damp panties. I feel her breath on me through the sheer fabric. I spread my legs a little wider, hoping she'll catch my drift. I want her. I want her more than I've wanted anything in my life. All the desire I've ever felt is compressed in this intense moment of longing. I don't know how she'll react, but the impulse is stronger than my resolve. I reach for the back of her head and press myself against her. I feel her hot lips on my clit, her warm breath on me, eliciting another moan from my throat.

"I want you. Please."

I let go of her head and cede all control. Her head doesn't move much. Her tongue skates along the gusset of my panties, halting at my clit. Then she slowly pushes my underwear to the side and waits a beat, as though she's staring at it, before covering my clit with her lips.

I press my palms against the wall for support. The pleasure is instantaneous, reaching out from deep within, spreading its tentacles. It's as though my orgasm is ready to erupt with every flick of her tongue, but it doesn't. Not yet. My body waits for me to catch up, for my mind to wrap itself around this.

I've only dreamt of this for decades. My core fantasy, my therapist called it. We all have one, she said, but most of us don't know what it is. We're either too afraid of it or too overwhelmed. You know what yours is. What are you going to do with it?

Here I am. Living my core fantasy. It exceeds the imagined version of it a millionfold. Fantasy has nothing on reality. Sharon's tongue swirls around my clit, and I know what will happen next. That's why I'm willing my orgasm to wait, even though it's knocking at the door more ferociously now. Sharon knows too. She's known everything since I confided in her a few months ago. She's the one who enticed me to start planning. And here I stand at the culmination of it all, all the details, the weeks of living apart, all for this moment. But it's not just this moment. This moment that will be the happy ending of a lived-out fantasy but also the beginning of something else. Something new. Of me no longer being afraid of my desire, giving voice to it, and making my fantasies come true. Because I have Sharon, who pushes herself up now, and who is no more a stranger to me than I am to myself.

She looks into my eyes, slides her hand into my panties, and slips a finger high inside of me.

It's more than enough to push me over the edge. Now that I'm looking at her beautiful, kind face—a face that I'd been taking for granted for too long before we did this.

Sharon fucks me, and I give myself to her, to this fantasy, completely. Tears stream down my cheeks as I come at her fingers, which are the least important part of all of this. They're the instrument that gets me there, experiencing a magnitude of pleasure new to me. It doesn't shoot up from my core the way it used to, but it originates from all over my body, little fires everywhere under my skin, in my flesh, even though they all ignite at her fingertips.

"I love you." I sag against her, my body weak from all the tension it has released.

Sharon holds me in her arms. She kisses my cheek, and I feel her lips stretch into a smile against my skin.

Despite my sheer exhaustion, I can't help but burst out into a chuckle. It's the decompression. The memory we have made for ourselves and the months of planning and the weeks of living apart just for this moment. But it was all worth it, every second of it.

Sharon nuzzles my ear. "Shall we do that again sometime?"

I don't say anything. I just hold her close. She can come home now, my Hot Blonde.

Help Yourself

Emma Weimann

Emily had been tossing and turning for more than two hours. While her body was exhausted, her mind was racing a hundred miles an hour and just wouldn't slow down, no matter how hard she tried.

The light snores coming from the other side of the bed didn't help.

Emily growled and put a pillow over her head. She loved Hannah. She really did. Only not tonight. Right now, all she wanted was to be alone and able to sleep.

As so often happened lately, her mind had sprung awake as soon as she'd switched the light off. Hannah's snores weren't the reason for her insomnia. Emily knew that. She also knew that she needed to go to sleep soon, since work tomorrow would be as hectic and demanding as it had been ever since her new boss had arrived. He was a class A jerk and had sought her out as the person he needed to torture to establish himself as the alpha beast in the office. So far, no reasoning had worked with him. Nothing she did was good enough. The work she had loved had turned into a nightmare, and sleep didn't come easily anymore.

These past nights she'd tried a lot of remedies, from drinking warm milk (disgusting), alcohol (hangovers were a pest), sports (really, really not her thing), and counting sheep (made her even more awake). Nothing had helped.

Well, nothing—except sex. Hannah's temperament and a few orgasms and cuddles afterward always made Emily fall asleep like a baby.

She took the pillow from her head and glanced over at the other side of the bed.

Moonlight painted her girlfriend in a soft white light. She was so beautiful with her blue eyes, blonde hair, and a body to die for.

Emily reached over and touched a silky strand of hair. *How have I gotten so lucky with you?* Hannah's body was a big turn on, yes, but had not been the reason Emily had finally caved and gone out on a date with a woman. She'd fallen for Hannah's humor, her intelligence, and big heart. Hannah was the one person that could make her laugh, make her think, and make her feel cherished. Before, sex had been sex: sometimes good, sometimes just a bad decision. But with Hannah, sex was so much more—it was fun and intimate, electrifying and relaxing. All in one. The whole package.

When Hannah looked at her with that special, predatory intensity, Emily turned into a mess of heat and hormones. She was addicted to her girlfriend's touch. A touch that was so soft and yet so often felt like fire licking over skin.

The thought of Hannah going down on her... A wave of heat rushed through Emily's body and hit her center.

Maybe Hannah wasn't *that* deeply asleep.

"Hey?" Emily whispered, while lightly touching Hannah's hand. "Are you awake?" She leaned on her elbow and looked into a sleep-relaxed face. There was no reaction at all.

Damn. Disappointed, Emily let herself fall back on the mattress. So sex was out of the question. What a shame.

She ran her finger over the duvet, about to accept her fate of another sleepless night.

Except. An idea popped into her head. She could fly solo. Something she hadn't done in a while—not since Hannah had started staying over regularly a few weeks ago. From that point on, Emily's sex life had taken a dramatic turn for the better. Being intimate with Hannah was better than a triple-chocolate brownie on a sunny day at the beach and even better than reading a new book by Emily's favorite author. And that said a lot.

Masturbating wasn't better or worse per se; it was...something completely different. Plus, unlike chocolate, an orgasm had no calories and, unlike alcohol, didn't leave a hangover. Also, it did burn calories, which even made it some kind of exercise. Right? Right.

Only, doing "it" with someone sleeping next to her felt a bit weird. Not that Hannah would mind. She would probably be fascinated and join in. Still, it would be embarrassing to get caught.

At least they didn't have a squeaky bed.

Carefully, Emily slipped one hand under the waistband of her pajama pants. The slickness underneath her fingers was testimony that all the thinking about Hannah and sex had not left her unaffected. She grinned and slowly ran a finger up her slit, then brushed it over her clit, gasping a little at the contact.

Hannah grumbled and moved.

Emily froze. *Shit.*

She didn't even dare to breathe when she cast a glance at the other side of the bed.

"You awake?" she whispered.

Light snores were her only answer.

Relief flooded Emily. Slowly moving the hand out of her pants, she grimaced. So much for masturbating to relax and find sleep. This was not the solution she was looking for.

She turned on her side and concentrated on the sounds around her, eyes closed. The refrigerator's hum seemed awfully loud in the stillness of the night. The creaking of furniture was followed by a floorboard's groan somewhere nearby. A sound that reminded her of one that Hannah made when kissed behind her ear. A very sensitive place.

Grumbling, she turned again and pressed the back of her head deeper into the fluffy pillow. Not only was she not able to sleep, she was still horny.

Should she give it another try?

The guest room. Emily barely stopped herself from groaning. Why hadn't she thought about this before? She would simply tiptoe into the guest room and let Hannah sleep in peace.

With a grin, she got out of bed. She hesitated, then quietly opened her nightstand drawer. Nestled between hand lotion and tissues was the box with her vibrator. Emily took it and left the bedroom.

The hall was bathed in semidarkness and tranquility. The whole place seemed like a different apartment at night. Shapes and forms were nothing but a reminder of furniture, and sounds were much louder than during daytime.

Something soft touching her leg nearly made her jump out of her skin. "Don't do that."

A meow was her answer.

"No, be quiet," Emily whispered.

The next meow reminded her of a horror movie scream. The sound nearly gave her a heart attack.

There was only one way to make sure that Monster didn't wake Hannah: food. Emily put the box with the vibrator on the sideboard and picked up her now-purring cat. She ran her finger through his fur. "You are a little dictator, you know that, right?"

The purring sounded a lot happier.

Cats!

Three minutes later, a happy furball was munching away on an after-midnight snack.

Satisfied that the cat was out of the equation, Emily smiled. With feet as cold as ice, she left cat and kitchen behind, picked up her box from the sideboard, and went into the guest room.

She closed the door behind her and put the box down on the nightstand. Being here felt weird. This room hadn't been used in a long time. Just like the vibrator. A lot had changed in her life; that was for sure.

Emily opened the box. Handling the device was self-explanatory and a bit like riding a bike—one never forgot. So she tossed the manual aside. However, the vibrator probably needed to be charged first, at least for ten minutes or so. There would be no joy in having the machine die on her just when she needed it to fulfill its job.

After plugging everything in, Emily looked around the room. The charging would take a while. Too long to use the time for foreplay. With a sigh, she went over to the window and gazed outside. The guest room had a view of the lake, which right now looked a bit like a dark mirror with the moon shining down on it.

She opened the window and breathed in the fresh, cool night air. A light breeze ruffled some leaves nearby. An owl hooted. This really was a nice area to live, especially in the summer.

The smell of the nearby lavender bush brought back memories of last Sunday. They had spent it at the old boathouse, with Peter and his plaything of the week. Fortunately, his new guy hadn't been half as stupid as the ones before, who had been nothing more than eye candy. This one was still in her brother's life, even in month two. Which was some kind of record.

After taking one last deep breath, she closed the window and leaned her forehead against the cool glass. She loved her brother but would never understand how siblings could be so different when it came to relationships. He had no problems sleeping around and enjoyed his lifestyle. She had only had three relationships in her life so far—two with guys and then with Hannah. Remembering how long Hannah had needed to court her before Emily had even realized what Hannah had been doing made her chuckle. *I was so clueless.*

She sat down on the bed. And yawned. This mattress actually wasn't half bad. A bit softer than the one in the master bedroom. She couldn't help yawning again and then shook her head. *No. No way.* She would not go to sleep right now. If she did, she would be asleep for a few minutes and then be shaken awake by some kind of nightmare. Wide awake until she had to get up for work. Her brain was a hyperactive bitch. What Emily needed was positive relaxation that would make her float into dreams as sweet as candy.

She got up again and wiggled her still-cold toes. The slippers were in the master bedroom, and she would not risk waking Hannah.

But there was something in the kitchen that would help cold feet. Red wine. An already open bottle of Shiraz was waiting for her in the kitchen.

Emily tiptoed through the hall and slipped back into the kitchen. A happily purring cat greeted her, jumped from his chair, went to his empty dish, and probably thought this night was some kind of cat heaven.

Emily shook her head. "No, no. First of all, you just had a snack. And secondly, I'm leaving again, right now." She took the bottle and a glass and left the room.

Monster followed her to the guest room, meowing miserably the whole way, the sound the equivalent of nails on a chalkboard.

"You're really trying to get me into a hell of a mess here, mister."

Another frightening meow was her answer. Never had she been happier that Hannah was a heavy sleeper. "No, go. Hunt mice or whatever you cats do in the middle of the night."

Emily melted under the expression of utter betrayal on her cat's face. "Ah, damn. Come in." She took a step back and watched him hurry across the room, only to jump on the bed. "No. Down." She rolled her eyes. Who was she fooling? Had anyone ever managed to make a cat do something?

Frustrated, she poured herself a glass of wine and put the bottle on the small side table. This was the last bottle of the pack of six a colleague had given her as a thank you for saving his sorry ass. If only she could save herself that easily at work.

Gently, she swirled the glass in tiny circles to allow the Shiraz to breathe. Its dark and rich smell made her mouth water. She took a sip and let the wine spread across her tongue, from front to back and side to side, before swallowing. It was a feast of flavors.

Emily sat next to her cat. "Do cats ever have problems sleeping?" She sighed. "Ever have a boss who abuses you, and you're seen as too passive to stand up for yourself?"

Monster didn't react at all.

"And even your girlfriend thinks you're a bit of a lost puppy, but that's so not true. No, it's not. Don't give me that skeptical look. I'm not that passive. I just want everyone to get along. Is that so ridiculous?"

Monster purred but otherwise didn't comment.

"Fine. I see that judgy face."

Monster turned on his back, paws in the air.

"You really do have the perfect life. You trained us humans exceptionally well, can sleep whenever and wherever you want, and you even have several lives." She rubbed her fingertips in small, circular motions near the cat's midsection. This was Monster's favorite spot, and the purr changed from that of a Volkswagen to one that sounded more like a small Ferrari.

"You would never want to swap with us humans, right?"

Monster squinted at her.

Emily chuckled. "Yeah, thought so. What I would give to be a cat." She emptied her glass. "Right, you're not going to like what's going to happen next." She unplugged the vibrator, put it on the nightstand, and slipped under the covers.

Monster got off the bed with an angry meow and jumped onto a chair at the other end of the room, glaring as only cats could, all hurt pride and murder.

Emily couldn't help but laugh. It seemed that even a cat's life wasn't all sunshine and belly rubs.

So, here she was. All alone. Well, as far as human company went. Now, how to get into the right mood again?

She put the vibrator next to her hip, within easy reach. A fantasy to turn her on was what she needed. Finding one wasn't difficult: Hannah, the woman who loved her and brought so much joy in her life. The woman with the amazing blue eyes and an ice-melting grin. A warm glow was starting in Emily's stomach.

She let her mind wander while she ran a finger over one of her nipples, remembering the first time Hannah had touched her intimately, the first time she had sucked on Emily's nipples. A shudder ran through her.

With a sigh, she put a bit more pressure on her finger and enjoyed the slow current running down from her nipples to her clit. *Nice. Yes.* That was more like it.

Her other hand joined in on the fun, and both nipples hardened while she treated them to a nice, slow, and sensual massage. She'd forgotten how much fun flying solo could be. Emily deliberately took her time to enjoy what she was doing, trying to savor the journey instead of hurrying toward the goal.

While her right hand stayed on her breast and continued the massage, she let her other hand wander down to stroke through her already wet curls. *Oh yes.* She inhaled deeply. This was nice. With a touch as soft as a butterfly, she put one finger on her clit, remembering how it felt when Hannah started to gently lick over her there.

A rush of moisture, paired with a wave of heat, was Emily's reward.

Time to up the game. She took the vibrator and switched it on to a low setting. Next, she put it on her pubic bone and gave herself a moment to get used to the sensations of the silicon on her body. And to give the silicon time to warm up a little. The tingling through her body increased. Emily took her time to move the vibrator down, slightly to the side of her clit. She sucked in a breath. *Yes. Yes.*

That did the job nicely.

Smiling, she ran her hand up her own thigh and let her mind wander freely, wherever it wanted to go. An image of her coming home early from a hard day at work popped into her mind and killed her mood slightly. But then the picture of Hannah appeared, already in bed. Naked. Waiting for her.

Emily sat down in the armchair next to the bed. Still fully dressed.

She imagined how Hannah would get out of bed to come and stand between her legs, all creamy white and beautiful. Emily would put her hands on Hannah's smooth skin and then run both hands up her body until she found the small patch of hair. All wet for her.

Emily increased the vibrator's speed slightly. All the pent-up tension, the cause for her insomnia, melted like ice cream on a tongue and slowly morphed into real excitement. She stifled a whimper when fantasy Hannah's fingers stroked through her wet curls and found Emily's fingers. Hannah took them and used them to stroke over her clit.

From one moment to the next, Emily was naked as well, still in the armchair. With a rough voice, she said, "Kneel down, hands behind your back. And use your tongue until I come."

Her eyes flew open. She switched the vibrator off, her clit still throbbing and asking for more. But where had this command come from? Why had she been fantasizing about telling Hannah what to do and expecting her to simply obey? Being compliant was Emily's nature. Being commanding was Hannah's.

She bit her lip. On the other hand… Maybe she should practice being more demanding. At least from time to time. And in her fantasy.

She could start tonight and see how it felt.

Taking a deep breath and letting the air go out of her lungs again, she closed her eyes and envisioned herself back in the armchair, with a wet Hannah in front of her and the armchair's rough texture under her naked ass.

"Kneel between my legs. Tease my nipples." Her voice was a bit shaky and the command a bit more a question…but it was a start. And it felt good.

With the trademark killer smile, fantasy Hannah obeyed. She carefully spread Emily's legs to kneel between them before reaching out to cup both her breasts.

Emily shivered. This touch, so soft and yet so sure, was what she craved. With trembling fingers, she switched the vibrator on again and positioned it on the outside of her lips. "Lick me."

Not hesitating for one moment, fantasy Hannah dipped her tongue between the folds and then trailed it up through Emily's flesh until she hit the small, swollen mound where all of Emily's lust and want were centered.

The touch was like fire, melting through to the other side.

Hannah's tongue circled her clit slowly while Emily let out small whispers, letting go. "More. Harder," she told fantasy Hannah.

Emily increased the vibrator's speed, enjoying how the pressure against her warm, throbbing pulse was gentle enough to still be pleasurable. Still, she needed more. "Use your fingers."

Two fingers slipped easily into slick heat, adding to the pressure that was building inside her.

"Oh…" Her breathing became erratic, arousal clawing its way up her spine and spreading through her whole body. "Make me come. Now."

The mattress beside her dipped.

Damn cat.

"How do you want me to make you come?"

For a second, Emily stopped breathing. Her eyes flew open.

"Tell me." Hannah sat on the bed, a wicked grin on her face.

"Shit…I'm sorry…I…" Emily pulled the duvet closer around her and considered spontaneous self-combustion. This moment won the competition of *most embarrassing moment ever* hands down.

"No. Don't be sorry. Just don't stop." Hannah's voice was barely more than a purr.

"I… I can't. This is…no."

"Please, Emily. I think this is one of the sexiest things I've ever witnessed in my life. You ordering someone around in your fantasy."

Sexy. Oh. "Not someone. You." Her face felt as if it were on fire.

"Really? Tell me. What did I just do?" Hannah brushed a strand of hair from Emily's face.

The touch sent shivers through her. "I… I can't." Still embarrassed, she looked down.

Hannah cupped her face, leaned forward, and brought their lips together, her tongue brushing Emily's bottom lip softly before letting go again. "Don't be ashamed. This is really, really sexy. Share your fantasy with me, please."

Emily decided to be brave and cleared her throat. "You were kneeling in front of me, naked. Licking me and using your fingers to fuck me."

Hannah sucked in a breath, her eyes wide. "I'm wet already. Don't stop."

Emily frowned. "Really?"

Hannah's hand disappeared under the duvet, landing on her hip before finding Emily's hand with the vibrator. "Please. Tell me what you and your little helper were up to."

"I... That was it. Then real you scared the hell out of me."

Hannah chuckled and got up from the bed. Slowly, she stepped out of her pajama bottoms. "So, I was naked, yes?"

Emily nodded. Seeing Hannah strip like that rekindled the fire that had been snuffed out by her surprise.

Moments later, buck naked Hannah stood in the middle of the room. "Like that?" She held her arms out and turned until she faced Emily again.

"Yes. Very much."

"And what did you do?"

"I was letting you lick me." The words were out of her mouth before she could stop them.

Arms still akimbo, Hannah said, "I had the impression that you didn't let me but ordered me to."

Emily swallowed around the lump in her throat. "Yes, I ordered you to lick me and finger-fuck me. And you were doing a great job."

Hannah burst out laughing. "Who knew that answering the call of nature in the middle of the night would turn into such a hot event?" She smiled at Emily. "The day you said yes to me asking for the hundredth time if you would go out with me was the happiest day of my life." She looked at Monster, still perched on the armchair, seemingly nonplussed by the spectacle in front of him. "I'm really sorry, furball," Hannah said, "but you have to find a new place from where to rule your kingdom. Your mama needs the chair." She picked the cat up, put him out in the hall, closed the door, and turned back to Emily. "I'm all yours. I'll follow your lead." And with those words, a naked Hannah stood next to the armchair, hands behind her back. "This is your show." She smiled. "If you want to."

"Do you want to?"

"You wouldn't believe how much."

Gathering all her courage, Emily got out from under the duvet. A part of her still hadn't grasped that this was happening for real. She licked her lips and closed her eyes, needing to get back into the role she had in her fantasy. "I'm also naked. I'm sitting in the armchair." She tried to remember how it had felt to give the commands. Her clit twitched when she remembered the image of Hannah's tongue touching her intimately. "You'll do as I say." Her voice sounded a bit rough and slightly unsure to her own ears.

"Yes. Always." The words were a breath on Hannah's lips. "Whatever you want."

Emily sat. The chair felt weird under her ass. Never before had she sat naked in an armchair. "Kneel between my legs, hands behind your back." She spread her legs, still feeling a bit uncertain.

Hannah moved fast. With her kneeling before Emily, they were nearly the same height.

Emily let her gaze travel down Hannah's body, her own body reacting to the sight. She reached out and cupped those wonderful breasts. Both nipples were already hard. A smile found its way to her face. "You like the idea of me ordering you around."

"Yes. Very much."

"And would you like to use your tongue on me, while I'm sitting here?" Emily ran her thumbs over Hannah's nipples.

Hannah made a keening noise in the back of her throat before she said, "Yes."

Something inside of her clicked in place. "Kiss me." She kept her fingers on those nipples, rolling them, teasing them, wanting to give as much pleasure as she received.

Hannah took a series of short breaths to focus. "Where do you want me to kiss you?"

Oh. Right. Orders had to be precise. "On my lips. Make me melt."

For a second, Hannah gazed at those lips, and then she moved in while Emily's fingers continued their play.

The kiss started slow, exploratory. Soon Emily opened her mouth, and their tongues touched and danced with each other. Every contact sent jolts of pleasure down to her clit. She increased the pressure of her thumbs on Hannah's nipples. With every moan she drew from Hannah, Emily became more and more aware of the power she held. And power was really, really sexy.

Emily broke the contact and pressed soft butterfly kisses to the corner of Hannah's mouth. "Stop, but stay."

Their foreheads touched.

"I'm so wet. You're going to find a river down there." And that was exactly what she wanted Hannah to do now. "Keep your hands behind your back and lick me until I come. Slowly. Take your time."

"Yes." Hannah moved a few centimeters back.

Emily put one leg over the arm of the chair to grant better access.

Then Hannah was on a mission and dipped her tongue between those folds.

Every thought went out of Emily's brain. Nothing could compare to this. Nothing. She bit her lip and pressed her back into the chair. "Oh my god." This marvelous, talented tongue teased her, touched her, and withdrew again. Emily writhed and moaned. When Hannah's tongue touched Emily's clit for the first time, she slammed her hands down on the armrests. "Don't stop. Don't stop."

Hannah growled.

The noise went through Emily as if an electric wire had been touched directly to her clit. Slow was overrated. "Make me come. Now."

The pressure inside her built and built until the throbbing become nearly unbearable. "Suck me."

There was no hesitation: Hannah sucked Emily's clit into her mouth.

Emily held her breath. For a moment. Then a high-pitched whimper escaped when she came undone. The world inside her exploded, her orgasm going on and on.

Her vision was blurry. She was dimly aware of Hannah still sucking. Emily groaned, "Stop. Please."

Hannah stopped.

Taking a deep breath to try and clear her head, Emily opened her eyes, staring into Hannah's. "I... That was... I can't move."

Hannah grinned. "That was amazing. You are amazing." Her hands were still behind her back.

"Kiss me. Slow. On my lips."

Hannah looked down at the area she had been feasting on moments ago.

"No," Emily said with a chuckle. "No. That is a no-go zone right now. The lips up here."

With the slow smile that Emily had fallen in love with, Hannah complied. Soft lips met hers.

Emily touched Hannah's shoulders. She needed to feel more of her, enjoying the soothing and arousing connection between them. "I'm boneless. You liquefied me," she whispered.

"I did my best. So, what do you want me to do now?" Hannah was still in her role.

Emily looked at the bed and then back at her girlfriend. "I want to cuddle. But I don't want to leave you hanging. You haven't come, and I'm pretty sure that you won't easily go to sleep for the"—she looked at the clock and sighed—"short time of sleep left to us."

"Well, there's still the vibrator."

"Yes." Emily grinned. "There is that." A different kind of desire was making her head fuzzy. She would love to watch Hannah masturbate.

With a groan, Hannah got up and held out her hand, only to draw Emily into her arms.

Their bodies were flush against each other.

"This was the hottest thing ever," Hannah said. "You are the hottest thing ever. Don't hide this side from me. Or from yourself."

"I'll try."

"Yes, please."

Both slipped under the duvet.

Hannah took the vibrator. "So, can I make a request?"

"Sure you can."

"Make me come with the vibrator, and tell me how you want me to fuck you the next time. Please." She switched the vibrator on and put it in Emily's hand.

A delighted thrill ran through her, as did the vibrator's soft buzz. Emily put her head on Hannah's shoulder and the vibrator on her girlfriend's lower stomach. "You mean the next time I'll top you?"

Hannah's "yes" sounded breathless and excited.

⁓ාౝ⁓

Sunshine was already streaming through the window when Emily stirred from her dreams, warm hands tracing her hips, a naked body pressed against her equally naked one.

"Good morning, sunshine." Hannah's voice was rough from sleep.

"Morning."

"You really live the life, you know?"

"What?"

"There's a vibrator somewhere on the bed, a nearly empty bottle of wine next to it, and a pussy between your legs."

Emily looked down the bed, and yes, there was Monster sleeping between her legs. The bedroom door was slightly ajar. "Let's not forget the naked woman in my bed."

"Yep, there is that."

They both laughed.

Hannah planted a kiss on Emily's shoulder before asking, "How are you feeling?"

"Like shit because of the one hour sleep I had." She grinned. "But it was worth every second of snooze time I missed."

"I had a lot of fun last night." Hannah's fingers trailed down until she found Emily's most tender spot between her legs. "But yes, a bit more sleep would have been cool."

Emily sucked in a breath, torn between wanting to escape the intimate touch or beg for more. Damn office job.

"You're still so wet. I hate that we have to get up and go to work." Hannah pouted and rubbed Emily's folds. "I want to taste you again and let you order me around some more. And then I want to eat scrambled eggs with you and watch something fun before you have your way with me again. You've been so stressed lately, and last night was so awesome. I don't want to adult today. And I don't want you to adult either."

Emily closed her eyes, stifling a groan. Those fingers were driving her crazy. She put her hand over Hannah's to stop the movement. Last night had been…different, liberating, and strange in a good way.

Hannah was her life. Her boss could bite her. She opened her eyes to find a soft gaze on Hannah's face. "Here's what you'll do," Emily said. "You will call work and tell them you're ill. I'll do the same. And then you'll wait for me in the shower, naked. Is that understood?"

Hannah's eyes widened and her pupils darkened. "Yes." She instantly climbed out of bed and left the room, probably in search of her phone.

Emily looked at Monster, who didn't seem too happy about all the ruckus. "That was a night I will never forget." She'd wait an hour and then call in sick. By then, her voice should be hoarse enough to fake a cold.

ERASING THE LINES

A Kelli and Nora short story

KD Williamson

Detective Kelli McCabe leaned to the side to get a better look at the line of people in front of them. She didn't bother glancing behind her. Those dumbasses didn't matter. "Fuck, I think we've moved less than a centimeter."

Gerald Travis shrugged. "Mmm, well, I told you we should've called ahead. We don't usually come here around this time."

The Dirty Cat, one of the best food trucks in Seattle, had gotten even more popular over the past year and a half. It seemed as if everyone wanted their tacos. "You do know that wouldn't have made much of a difference?" Kelli glared at her partner and waited for him to say something else stupid or smartassy.

"Bullshit. He knows us. We coulda walked straight up to the window and picked it up." Travis crossed his arms. "We might have to Taco Bell it. We don't have a lot of time."

"Oh, hell no. Definitely not." Kelli pulled on the lanyard around her neck to make sure her detective shield was visible and adjusted her jacket accordingly. She grabbed Travis's arm and pushed her way through the line. "C'mon."

"What are you doing?"

"Using your idea. We're moving up."

People around them grumbled, but she held up her shield, hoping to keep shitty attitudes under wraps. It worked.

"Just like a damn cop abusing their power," someone called out.

Well, her plan almost worked. At least it got them past the middle part of the line. Kelli bit the inside of her cheek to keep from responding.

Travis sighed and ran a hand over his bald head. It was pretty much a new look for him, and it went well with his baby smooth face. No matter what he thought, Travis didn't look like a younger version of Kojak. If Travis's skin had been a lighter brown, then maybe.

"Don't they have crimes to stop or something?" the man behind them yelled.

Exactly. They did have crimes to solve, so he could just fuck right off and cut them a little slack.

"This is your tax money at work, everybody!"

People in front of them glanced at them.

"Goddammit, McCabe. You're about to start a riot over tacos," Travis muttered, a grin curling his lips.

She smiled back at him. "Probably."

Someone tapped Kelli on the back. She turned around, meeting one of the disgruntled people face-to-face. He should have chosen Travis. Sunshine usually came out of his ass, and Kelli sure as hell wasn't in the mood.

The man's eyes widened. "Uhhh."

The grumbles from behind him grew louder. The man took a step closer as if he drew energy from the crowd. "You cut in front of me."

"Yeah, I did." Kelli was very matter of fact.

"Well, you can't just ignore me."

"I heard every word you said, and I gotta tell you it's just tacos. So get over yourself."

The man's face reddened. Kelli didn't wait to see if he had anything else to say. She turned back to her stolen place in line.

Travis laughed. "Damn, woman. Look at you. Always making friends and influencing people."

Kelli shot him the finger.

"Use your words, McCabe."

"Okay, then. Fuck you." She smiled.

"That's better."

Kelli rolled her eyes.

"So what's making you surlier? The stakeout we have to do? Because I gotta remind you, it's our case. He robbed and killed an old lady for fuck's sake. I don't want a couple uniforms busting it wide open. We need to get there and claim what's ours. Or is the attitude more about Nora being out of town?"

Kelli had no doubt that their asshole shooter would show up at his ex-girlfriend's house. She was lying about what she knew; that much was obvious. Still, Travis just had to bring Nora up. She hadn't thought about her in a whole five minutes, which had all passed while she moved them closer to heaven in the form of carnitas tacos. Kelli glanced at him. "What do you think?"

"I think I can't wait for her to come back so your ass will be normal. But I can hang on for another forty-eight hours."

"Yeah, don't remind me." Two days. Two more fucking days. Kelli wasn't sure that she could last that long, but it wasn't as if she had a choice. Nora was in goddamn California. Part of Kelli was proud of Nora for branching out. As a surgeon, Nora had never been to a medical conference before. Change had painted them both, just with different brushes. Nora's horizons had broadened, whereas Kelli's edges had softened. Minutely, anyway. All the irritation that had taken hold of her fizzled out. She missed Nora big time, and for the moment, there wasn't room for anything else. Two more days might as well have been two weeks. They talked, texted, and used just about every other fucking digital device or program to close the distance, but it wasn't anywhere near enough. Hell, even Phineas, Nora's pet kune kune, was acting funny. He wasn't being as social, and that was saying a lot for a two-hundred-pound pig with fur.

The line had thinned out somewhat in the past few minutes, leaving only two people ahead of them.

"Still going to see Tony this weekend?"

Kelli stared at Travis. She definitely didn't want to think about her dunderheaded younger brother spending the next decade in prison. Maybe while he was inside, his drug addiction would get better, not worse. "Was that your idea of a subject change?"

Travis shrugged. "We could talk about who Sean's fucking."

She cringed. "Uck, no."

He laughed. "He's your brother. You should care. Never know. She might be special."

"Uh-huh."

They stepped forward.

"Travis and McCabe! Why didn't you just call ahead? I would've done a pick up for you guys." Julio smiled at them.

Kelli met Travis's gaze. He pressed his lips together, closed his eyes, and shook his head.

"Use your words, Gerald."

Instead, he gave her the finger.

Kelli wrestled out of her jacket and threw it in the backseat. She licked a napkin and then rubbed it against her T-shirt, trying to get habanero sauce off the material before it stained. The shit was hot enough to burn a hole in concrete. She was surprised that her chest wasn't smoking.

"Good thing you weren't wearing a pantsuit," Travis said from the driver's seat.

"No point in being well dressed for a stakeout." The guy they were looking for was a first-time killer and lifelong thief. The amount of evidence he left at the crime scene could have been seen from space. So that made him stupid too.

"Hmm, I don't know, sometimes the cut of those suits makes you look intimidating as hell."

"Whatever," Kelli snorted. Clothes could make the woman, but her favorite thing? The way Nora looked at her when she walked into the kitchen dressed for work. Oftentimes that look sent them right back into the bedroom or, hell, even on top of the counter. A scalding heat churned in Kelli's stomach and seeped its way outward. Had it only been a week since Kelli had touched her? Jesus Christ, Nora brought out the horndog in her, and right now, that dog was starting to pant.

The phone calls, FaceTime, and Skype sessions were filled with a lot more than talking. Kelli bit her lip to keep from smiling. Nora was by no means a prude, but Kelli had no idea her freak flag flew that high. For lack of a better word, Nora was shameless, displaying and touching herself in ways that left Kelli's head spinning. The thought wrenched her stomach into pleasurable knots and made her sex clench. Kelli pressed her legs together to ease the growing tension.

Travis burped.

Kelli turned sharply to look at him in the semidarkness. Hell, she almost forgot she wasn't alone. Talk about potent.

"What?"

"Nothing."

"Uh-huh."

On top of the dashboard, Kelli's phone vibrated and lit up. She reached for it, and the pressure between her thighs jumped up several notches. Thank goodness it wasn't a request for FaceTime. Kelli had no idea which part of Nora's body would greet her. "Hey, you in for the night?"

"Yes, although I do believe I disappointed several colleagues by not attending the dinner party."

"Uh, you mean disappointed as in they were—"

"Propositioning me, yes."

"That's kinda hot," Kelli whispered. She glanced at Travis because she felt his smirk. He looked straight at her.

"Good thing I brought earphones. Tell Nora hi for me." He pressed the earbuds in.

Kelli cleared her throat. "Travis says—"

"I heard him. Now, what's hot about it?" Nora sounded confused but curious as well.

Shifting gears again wasn't hard given the way Kelli's body simmered. "That they want you and can't have you."

"No, they can't." Nora's tone was forceful, and it did something to Kelli's insides.

Two days. Two more fucking days. Kelli's mind scattered a bit, so she expressed the first thought that was clear. "You order something fancy from room service?"

"I'm not hungry, and you're changing the subject." Nora's voice deepened.

"Didn't mean to. Maybe part of me is trying to keep the conversation PG." Kelli licked her lips. She was on the job after all, and it needed to stay that way.

"What if I don't want it to be?"

Kelli sucked in a surprised breath and cut her gaze toward Travis. He bobbed his head to music turned up a lot louder on his cell phone than it needed to be. "I say I should probably give you what you want then." On the inside, Kelli cringed. What the hell was she doing? Going through with this phone call was far from the smartest thing to do.

"Good. I take that to mean that Travis is occupied?"

"Sounds like he's listening to the Foo Figh—"

"I don't care if it's *La Bohème.*"

Damn. That statement was way sexier than it had any right to be. No, Kelli wasn't being smart at all, but she was going to do it anyway. The apprehension prickling in Kelli's gut hiked up her excitement, and judging by the desperation in Nora's voice, this wasn't going to take long. Thank goodness she wasn't alone. Kelli had to believe she'd make a better choice otherwise.

"My sex drive has always been rather high, but with you, no matter how many times you're inside me…no matter how deep or hard, I want more," Nora continued, her voice low and seductive in a way that pulled Kelli in further.

While a section of Kelli's brain overloaded, other parts of her stood up and applauded. "Jesus, Nora."

"Every time I masturbated this week with you, for you, I still woke up in the middle of the night wanting more." Nora's tone was thick and her breathing ragged.

"Why didn't you call me?"

"It's not the real thing, is it? The way you feel, smell, taste…"

"God, I know what you mean." Kelli groaned.

"But I still want you to see and hear what you do to me. I have two days left, and I don't want to stop. Is that normal?"

"Normal isn't the right word. It's just us."

"I pulled up my skirt and brought myself to orgasm before calling you. I haven't even taken off my shoes yet."

Images flashed through Kelli's head of Nora with her brown eyes closed, long blond hair and clothing disheveled but still in outrageously expensive heels as she groaned and rubbed her fingertips against her clit. Kelli's breath left her, and she didn't even bother to try to catch it. Guilt shot through her. "Stop. We have to stop. Travis is—" She glanced at her partner.

He was still shaking his head, but his focus was on the house they'd been watching.

As if sensing her gaze, Travis turned toward her. He removed one of the earpieces. "What?"

"Nothing."

Travis continued to stare. "I'm not listening."

"I didn't say you were."

"The seats aren't waterproof."

Kelli punched him in the shoulder.

Travis laughed and put the earphones back in.

"You have to stop, but *I* don't," Nora said.

Dear God. In a few hours, Travis was going to look over and find her dead, crunchy, and dehydrated. "W-what?"

"I need you to understand what it feels like to want you like this."

"But I do." Kelli fidgeted.

"I don't think so, but you will. I've told you more than once that it can't always be about you."

"I know that, but this isn't the best time or place. I think Travis'll notice me fucking myself silly."

"Then, obviously that's not something you can do," Nora said.

"So, wait. You really think I can sit here and listen to you and not go off like a goddamn rocket?"

"You're a detective. You like being challenged."

"Damn right, I do."

"I'm glad we're on the same page. Besides, it should make your stakeout more interesting."

That it would, but interesting wasn't the right word. It was sugar coating. Regardless, Kelli still wasn't deterred.

"I don't think you have any idea how fucking hot you are when you talk like this." Kelli's breathing became uneven. She stared at the house across the street, wishing that things were about to go down instead of potentially embarrassing herself in front of her partner.

"I know what it does to you, and that's all that counts." Nora paused. "I just sent you a text. I thought it would be a safer option."

Shit. Nothing about this was safe, which made it, fuck, all the better. "He's right next to me, Nora."

"Then don't let him see." Nora's tone was sultry, thick.

Kelli pulled the phone away from her ear and opened the message. A picture of one of Nora's breasts greeted her in all its pink-nippled glory. When had she gotten undressed? Another photo followed of the same breast, but this time her nipple was erect and wet. Kelli forgot how to breathe. She licked her lips, knowing, remembering what Nora felt like in her mouth and on the back of her tongue. Then her recognition went deeper. Kelli brought the phone back to her ear, only to hear a whimper followed by sucking sounds. Even though it didn't have far to go, Kelli's stomach twisted and fell to the car floor.

"Christ." The word came out of Kelli's mouth in a growl. "You—you're trying to kill me." She didn't expect Nora to answer right away. Her mouth was full.

Yet another text arrived. Kelli shifted toward the passenger side window, turning as far away as she could before she even glanced at it. Nora's tongue circling her own nipple. Kelli's chest heaved in an effort to breathe. Something in her short-circuited, sending an electric tingle all over her body, settling between her thighs. She pressed her legs together tightly and grabbed hold of the passenger assist handle above her. Kelli was going for a ride. She needed to hang on.

"It's nowhere near the same as when you do…it." Nora moaned, but it was muffled. The one thing she heard clearly was the rapid flicking of Nora's tongue.

"I imagine not, but it sounds like you're doing a bang-up job of trying." Kelli swiveled her hips to find a more comfortable position, but with everything going on between her legs at the moment, that was damn near impossible. "Are you dreaming about us when you wake up in the middle of the night?"

"Yes." Nora's voice was distant but no less needy. Kelli wondered what she was doing and waited for visual evidence to pop up.

"Tell me," Kelli said.

"It's a variation of the same dream. You're on your knees behind me—"

"Spanking you?"

Nora made a small noise, and the covers rustled. "At...times." She sounded pained.

"You're wet as hell right now, aren't you?"

"Yes." Nora dragged the word out.

"Let me help you with that." If Kelli had to sit there and take it, she wasn't going to make things easy on Nora. Not at all. "You should see how red your ass gets. It's like your skin is on fire. All I wanna do is rub myself all over you."

"You do." Nora's voice shook.

"I know. What does it feel like to have my clit sliding over your ass like that?" Kelli leaned her head against the window.

Nora swallowed so hard it might have been a gulp. She followed up with a throaty, desperate sound. "Like...you're all over me at once, and I can't get away from it." She paused. "I don't want to get away from it."

"Next time, I'm gonna take a video so you can see. Then you can take it with you wherever you go."

"I don't think that's a good i-idea."

"Yes, it is, and I have an even better one. Touch yourself."

Kelli heard rustling again and wondered if Nora was on top of the covers or underneath. Experience told her Nora was on top of them, naked with her legs spread wide.

"No." That one word was succinct, sexy, and final. It was also a definite challenge.

"You're trying to drag this out. Make me lose my shit. This *is* about me," Kelli said.

The only thing Kelli heard on the other end was labored breathing, which was all the answer she needed. "Since I'm on my knees, do you dream about me fucking you in the ass too?"

Nora gasped.

"With or without the strap on?"

"Does it matter?" Nora's voice trembled.

"You know it does."

"With."

82

"Yeah, you do like that an awful lot. I'm so glad you told me you'd done it before. You were so quiet at first, but then you couldn't stop moaning my name. Then you started touching yourself and wanted me to go harder, faster."

"Yes."

"Yes, what?"

"I remember," Nora said.

"So how's that wetness problem at this point?" It was quiet on the other end. "Hello?"

Kelli's phone vibrated against her face.

"I'm sure you'll let me know if the evidence is substantial enough, Detective."

Every single muscle and nerve below Kelli's waist twitched. Nora was trying to turn the tables on her, and for some reason that shifted Kelli's arousal to somewhere in space. "Jesus fucking Christ."

"Pardon me?"

"I didn't say anything."

"I'm waiting for an answer," Nora said.

Travis cleared his throat and fidgeted. Kelli glanced his way, but he was only reaching for his drink.

Their eyes met.

He raised a brow.

She scowled. Pissed that she was here. Pissed that *he* was here. Pissed she wasn't in Nora's bed, deep inside her. All of that should have been a deterrent, but the truth of the matter was that it turned her on more. Instead of pressing her thighs together, Kelli opened them. The temptation to rub herself off on the seam of her pants was getting a little too real.

Kelli pulled the phone from her ear. The text app was still open. Kelli's mouth fell open as she stared at a picture of Nora, swollen, pink, and incredibly aroused. Nora's hand rested against the neatly trimmed patch of blonde hair, but her fingers were pointed downward in a V, holding her labia wide open.

Everything between Kelli's legs felt as if it had been doused in flame. Helpless, she gripped the side of her seat and leaned forward as her sex clenched at nothing but air. All of her body processes stopped and came roaring back in one mighty whoosh. She pressed her lips together to keep from making noise because it wouldn't have been a whimper, more like a fucking scream. Then, before she could find a way to contain herself, another image appeared. Nora's hand position had changed. Two of her fingertips pressed against her clit.

Kelli's mind blanked. She had to get out of this car and go somewhere she could cry out while she fucked herself raw. But her only movement was to bring her cell phone back to her ear. The rational part of her brain ordered her to end this, but its voice was so small and feeble compared to the roaring inside her.

Nora's breathing was rough and loud. Kelli closed her eyes and listened, waiting and wanting more.

"Was it?" Nora asked on the tail end of a soft cry.

Staring out of the window into nothingness, Kelli opened her mouth to answer. Now, if she knew what the hell Nora was talking about. "Huh?"

Nora went quiet again, but seconds later, she chuckled. She goddamned chuckled. The sound was dirty and full of knowledge. Nora knew she'd wrested control away from Kelli and was smooth as hell while she did it. God, Kelli loved her even more because of it. "Evidence enough?"

Clarity came back, and Kelli let it in. "Fuck, yes. Are you still touch—"

"No, I—"

"Why?" The urgent tone in her voice didn't bother Kelli a bit.

"I don't want this feeling to end, and if I keep going—"

"You won't be able to stop."

"Yes, I want this to last."

"Oh God," Kelli groaned. "I don't know if *I* can get through this."

"You can and you will."

"I swear to God, if I move the wrong way, I'm gonna come hard enough to blast the roof off this car." Kelli balled her free hand into a tight fist.

"Look at Travis."

"What? Why?" Kelli cut her gaze his way.

"Consider him a coolant of sorts."

"He's the only thing keeping my hands out of my pants."

"I don't think that's a mantle he'd want."

"Goddammit, Nora, he's the last thing on my mind right now."

"I know." Nora paused. "Kelli?"

"Yeah?"

"I want to go inside."

Kelli's vision grayed, and she was a step away from hyperventilating. She took careful, deep breaths through her nose. How the fuck did Nora do that? Turn her on so completely, taper it off, and then do it all over again with a few words. "Do it."

Nora's moan was long, drawn-out, and visceral. The sound cut through Kelli, leaving her in pieces. "I…" Nora tried to speak, but the only thing that came out was a high-pitched sob.

Kelli's world tilted back and forth, completely fucking up her equilibrium. Then it was as if she was in a tunnel and everything around her disappeared, except for Nora's voice bouncing off the walls, magnified. She pressed the phone to her ear hard enough to leave an imprint. The sounds of Nora's pleasure quieted somewhat, becoming muffled and faint.

"Nora?"

There was no answer, so Kelli just listened. Nora's moaning became background noise, a soundtrack introducing the main event. Sliding in and out of wetness had a sound, a distinct one, and it took center stage. Kelli reared back into her seat, while inside, she flailed.

Travis looked her way, but Kelli reached for her drink and slurped on it hard in an attempt to play it off. Her head felt as if it might pop off her shoulders, and her heart beat so hard that catching her breath again was going to be damn near impossible. Kelli turned away from Travis and almost cried out when she closed her legs as a wave of pleasure hit her hard enough to drown her. She leaned against the passenger side door and continued to greedily take in every sound that greeted her.

"You hear it…don't you?" Nora's voice was a combination of confidence, arousal, and need.

Kelli closed her eyes again. "Yeah."

"Yes, what?"

"I hear it."

"Sometimes you…" Nora swallowed hard, and her breathing was in tatters. "Have no patience, and you just pound into me."

Kelli bit her bottom lip and sucked it into her mouth in hopes that the sting would give her some sort of relief. The pain pushed her up a notch. "You like that."

"No. Love it, but—"

"Then do it."

Nora sucked in a breath and let it out filled with words. "Yes! Fuuuu…"

That one word, no matter how abbreviated, falling from Nora's lips nearly separated Kelli from her body. "If you were here right now, I'd let you do whatever you wanted. Fuck me in as many ways as—"

"God! I—" Nora's words were cut off by a loud, throaty moan.

The sound caught Kelli by surprise. She knew it well. It weaved its way around her, and she hung on as it tried to wring an answering orgasm from her. Kelli gritted her teeth. It felt as if she shook on the inside. "Shhhit."

Nora countered with broken whimpers.

At the moment, Kelli could lift a tank, but at the same time, she was too weak to stand. Every neuron fired, and it was as if she could not only feel it but see it as well. Air crackled against her skin, causing goosebumps and tingles.

"Kelli?"

"Mmm?"

"You're still with me?"

"I should be asking you that, but, yeah, I'm here. Barely." Kelli eased back in her seat.

The slide of the covers as Nora moved couldn't have been any louder. The sound made Kelli miss her all the more.

"Do you understand now?"

Kelli huffed and smiled, even though her body was one big nerve. She could take on the world and get lost in it at the same time. It was a heady feeling, but it wasn't new to her. "I always did. I feel it too."

"Good. I miss you."

"Miss you too. Just two more days."

"Two days."

"Awww!"

Kelli damn near broke her neck turning toward Travis.

He took an earbud out. "I don't know what she just said to you, but I love the goofy-ass look on your face."

She glared at her partner. Kelli could see him just fine with the help of the light from her phone.

Travis smiled, baring his teeth. "Moist towelette?"

The sudden sound of Nora's laughter shocked Kelli.

"You should probably take him up on that offer," Nora said.

Kelli sputtered and shook her head, but she couldn't help the chuckle that escaped. "I can't believe you just said that."

"What? What did she say? I wanna laugh too." Travis leaned toward Kelli, but she gave him a shove.

Travis grinned.

Kelli pushed him harder. He laughed and swatted at her, but her mood was so much better. As if she had a choice in the matter. Nora took care of that. "Don't hang up."

"I wasn't planning on it."

"Good." Finally able to concentrate, Kelli turned her attention back toward the house. All shit was right with the world, or at least, it was as close as it could be.

∞⌇⌇∞

If you enjoyed this short story, check out *Blurred Lines* by KD Williamson, the novel in which Nora and Kelli met and fell in love.

HOUSESHARE

A.L. Brooks

Kat hesitated on the doorstep. The front door to the impressive building was imposing, and none of this added up. She gazed up at the perfectly finished façade, the Georgian windows looking very much like they were originals, the brickwork impeccable. This house, like most in this part of London, screamed money, so why on earth was the rent being charged for the room so low?

Nel's words came back to her. "There's a catch. There has to be."

They'd poured over the ads online, trying to read between the lines of each one, and although they both kept coming back to this one for reasons they couldn't explain, they both had doubts.

"No one rents out a room that cheaply in that area. It sounds like some kind of human trafficking or prostitution trap to me." Nel looked serious, and that didn't happen often.

Kat had agreed with her, and they'd moved on to other ads. But later that night, when she was tossing and turning on Nel's sofa, the ad came back to her. It was the quality of the language used and the fact they hadn't tried to keep within the "thirty words for free" limit the website offered. The ad had run to nearly treble that and used full sentences with proper punctuation.

Kat was a sucker for proper punctuation.

So, without telling Nel, she'd e-mailed the owners of the Georgian terrace in Pimlico. After an initial phone call with a woman who sounded very pleasant and certainly not like a human trafficker, as far as Kat could tell, they had arranged for Kat to view the room.

As she stood on the doorstep in the late Friday evening sunshine, Kat's resolve was giving way to the doubts she'd had all along. No, this was crazy. Time to face up to the horrendous mistake she was about to make and turn tail.

She had taken one step backwards when the door swung open. Kat stared at the woman revealed by the opening door and only just resisted the urge to look skywards as the words *you have got to be kidding me* screamed inside her head.

The woman standing before her was tall, maybe six inches taller than Kat, who was no shorty at 5'7". She had long, straight, black hair that fell around her bare shoulders. Her eyes were a piercing green, her face slightly angular but classically beautiful. The green strapless dress she wore hugged her body and emphasised full breasts and wide hips. And she smiled knowingly at Kat, as the recognition was clearly mutual.

Kat had crushed on this woman for about a year now. She'd spotted her at the various women-only clubs and bars around London that she'd gone to with Nel, and Kat had been mesmerised from afar. Up close, the impact the woman had on her was nothing short of shocking. Kat couldn't breathe, and the sly smile the woman sported wasn't helping. The confidence she had in what she was doing to Kat was written across her face and made Kat squirm in discomfort.

"You must be Kat," the woman said. "I'm Claire. I believe you spoke to my partner, Veronica."

Of course, the partner. The equally stunning woman Kat had seen Claire draped over whenever Kat had run into them. Just as tall, with black skin that contrasted so perfectly with the whiteness of Claire and long, silver braids. When pressed together, they looked like a negative version of each other, and the effect was eye-popping. Kat knew she wasn't the only one staring any time they were out together.

And that meant the woman whom Kat had laughed and joked with on the phone two nights ago was Veronica. She shook her head as disbelief turned into mortification—she'd cracked a couple of her cheesiest self-deprecating jokes on that call. Veronica must think she was an idiot, and she'd think that even more when she came face-to-face with Kat.

Kat groaned. "Er, yes. Kat." She swallowed. "Sorry, I think I've made a mistake." She backed away.

Claire raised her eyebrows. "Mistake? How?" Her tone was cool but carried a hint of puzzlement.

Kat nodded. "Yes, sorry. I should go."

"Kat? Is that you?" Another voice came from down the hallway behind Claire, and soon Veronica came into view. She looked amazing, of course, in a long jersey dress that stopped just above her knees. Her braids were loosely tied back, leaving her perfect face on display. "Oh, great. You're here." She held out her hand. "Hi, I'm Veronica, but you can call me Ronnie."

Kat shook the proffered hand on autopilot.

"Except," Claire said coolly, "Kat was just leaving. Apparently."

Ronnie looked from Kat to Claire and back again. "Kat? Is there a problem?"

Kat sighed. Well, this was going splendidly, wasn't it? How desperate was she for a room? Sure, Nel's sofa wasn't the most comfortable living arrangement, but she could suffer it a little longer, couldn't she? At that thought, she instantly backtracked. No, she needed her own place. As much as it had been lovely of Nel to step in and offer Kat some space once things finally went pear-shaped with Paul, it had been two months now. It was time, for sure, but was this situation going to be any improvement? Yes, Claire and Ronnie offered more than a lumpy sofa to sleep on—she hoped—but this scenario could be equally uncomfortable, albeit for very different reasons.

Crushing on both your landladies could be awkward.

But their ad had been the best by far. By way far. How long could Kat keep looking for a new home? Nel was being polite, but Kat also knew their friendship was being stretched, as Kat's presence in Nel's flat was cramping Nel's style. And just because Kat thought both Claire and Ronnie were attractive—such a tame word for what they were—didn't mean she couldn't control any lustful thoughts she might have about them. And they were a couple, so it wasn't as if there was a risk of anyone getting silly about anything. She nearly laughed out loud—as if either of these two goddesses would deign to even look at Kat, never mind get tempted for any shenanigans with her.

That settled it.

"Sorry, no. No, there isn't. I'm… Oh, never mind. Could I come in?" Kat gave them her most winning smile and crossed her fingers behind her back. To her relief, after one flick of a glance between them, Claire and Ronnie both nodded.

The house was like something out of a glossy lifestyle magazine. It oozed class from every corner. It was furnished in a contemporary style that somehow worked perfectly with the original Georgian features. Kat's jaw dropped as she was led from one stunning room to another. She barely registered what the two women told her about the house and its rooms and knew she'd simply have to embarrass herself later and ask them to repeat it all.

Finally, they walked into a large kitchen, and Claire gestured Kat into a chair.

"Tea? Coffee? Something stronger?" Claire smirked, and Kat's own mouth shot into a smile as if by some Pavlovian response. "We have a rather delicious Pinot Noir open for the evening."

"Er, yes. Wine would be d—lovely." God help her, she'd nearly said *wine would be divine.*

Claire nodded, her smile widening, and as she poured out three glasses of wine, Ronnie slipped into the chair next to Kat. Her proximity allowed Kat to breathe in her perfume; it was earthy, musky, and conjured up images of running naked in a forest after rain.

Kat took the glass Claire offered her, and the three women clinked glasses before enjoying the first sip. It was smooth and rich, and Kat let it roll over her tongue and around her mouth before swallowing. Definitely an improvement on the five-quid supermarket brand she normally treated herself to on a Friday night.

What are you doing here, Kat? This place, these people are way out of your league.

"So, Kat, it's good to finally meet you properly." Ronnie's voice was as smooth as the wine—not deep but melodious, rolling over Kat like a length of silk. She sunk a couple of inches down in her chair as parts of her melted at the sound.

"And you," she said.

Ronnie smiled. She stared at Kat, and there was a sparkle to her eyes that made the nerves in Kat's spine tingle.

"We just have a few questions, and then we'll show you the room that's available." Claire pulled her chair a little closer to Kat's.

Her scent also reached Kat's nose. It was more floral than Ronnie's but not overpoweringly so. It was light and delicate and somehow offset some of the sharpness of Claire, softening her edges. Her eyes, too, sparkled as they gazed down on Kat. It should have been intimidating, being so close to these women, being the centre of their undivided attention, but, instead, Kat found herself basking in it, revelling in the intoxicating warmth of their proximity.

After twenty minutes of fairly intense but non-invasive questioning, plus a full glass of the wine, Kat was rather relaxed. She couldn't stop smiling, and parts of her body continually tingled, as if she were in the presence of an electrically charged force field.

"One last question," Ronnie said.

"Sure, ask away." Kat waved a hand in the air. She was so comfortable in their presence, in this situation, she would happily answer anything.

"Well, as we've made clear from the ad, Claire and I are in a relationship. Do you have any issues sharing a house with two lesbians?"

Kat couldn't help her snort. "No, not at all! My friend, Nel, whose sofa I'm currently sleeping on, is lesbian, and I'm bi. So, no, no problem at all."

"Excellent." Claire almost purred the word. "And I think that explains why we've seen you out and about."

Kat blushed but nodded. "Yes, Nel and I often hit the clubs together. I'm her wingwoman. I am, er, was seeing a guy called Paul, but most Fridays I'd go out with Nel and make sure she didn't go home with some nutter."

Ronnie chuckled. "Hm, yes, unfortunately there are a few of them out there."

"Oh God," Kat said, "tell me about it! And Nel always seemed to attract them." She rolled her eyes, and they all shared a laugh.

"Recent breakup?" Claire's voice was gentle.

Kat blinked. Oh, right, Paul. "Yeah. About two months ago. We'd been together about a year, but it never quite worked how it should. Always something to fight about." She shrugged. "It's the right thing to have ended it, but I realise now we should have done it sooner. I kind of miss him but don't all at the same time."

Ronnie nodded. "It'll take time, I'm sure. A year's a long time to be with someone and then suddenly not be." She reached out a hand and placed it carefully over Kat's where it lay on her own thigh. Ronnie's fingertips brushed—deliberately or inadvertently?—at the stocking-covered skin just below the hem of her skirt, and although featherlight, the touch seemed to reach deep into Kat. In the next moment, Claire placed a warm hand on Kat's shoulder and squeezed. Through the thin material of Kat's shirt, the heat of Claire's palm scorched her so intensely Kat would not be surprised to see a handprint left behind when she inspected her skin later.

Kat blinked, her gaze moving slowly from Ronnie to Claire. They smiled in a way that was simultaneously sympathetic and…a tad predatory, Kat realised with a start. *What the—?*

"So are you ready to see your room?" Ronnie's voice broke into Kat's thoughts, and the removal of Ronnie's hand from her thigh snapped her to attention.

"Room? Oh, yes." Kat was tempted to slap herself in the head—what was wrong with her? Instead, she stood as soon as Ronnie gave her room to do so and flexed her arms and shoulders a little to pull herself out of her daze. For one crazy moment, she wondered if they'd drugged the wine, but she pulled that thought up sharp. No, she definitely had her usual faculties all in working order. It was simply the presence of the two women who now guided her out of the kitchen that had her wits in a scramble. Their magnetism, for want of a less cheesy word, was a hard force to resist.

She followed them along a wood-floored hallway and up a carpeted staircase.

"This is our room." Claire pointed at an open doorway to her left as they rounded the top of the stairs.

Kat saw an opulent room, all reds and golds, and a messy, unmade bed. It seemed incongruous with the two immaculately presented women on each side of her. Who knew goddesses forgot to make their bed?

"And this would be yours." Ronnie took a gentle hold of Kat's elbow and steered her down the hall to the room next to theirs.

Kat blinked as she realised how close she would be sleeping to the pair. Would she hear them? Would the noise of their lovemaking reach her ears as she tried to sleep? Could she bear the torture if it did?

"Well, what do you think?" Claire sounded offended at Kat's lack of response, but she had to swallow hard before answering.

The room they had led her to was...magnificent. There was no other word for it. The bed was a king-size, a dark wood frame with impressive half posts on each corner and covered in a beautiful sage green duvet and pillows to match. The walls were papered with something that looked like silk in a pale green shot through with gold threads. The cream carpet was lush, and the additional furniture—a huge wardrobe and an old-fashioned dresser—were of the same dark wood as the bed. Two large windows hung with voluptuous green drapes would let in significant light during the day. It was stunning, and Kat felt completely and utterly out of place.

"It's...it's incredible," she whispered. She faced them. "I don't understand. How come it's so cheap?" She hadn't meant to be so crass in asking that one burning question, but it was out there now with no way to take it back.

Ronnie chuckled, and Claire rolled her eyes.

"We're not in it for the money," Claire said.

"Well, what then?" Kat asked. It was getting down to the nitty-gritty now; she needed to know what game they were playing because there sure as hell had to be one.

"Let's call it companionship." Ronnie smiled in a way that Kat supposed was meant to reassure. It made Kat even more nervous.

She quirked an eyebrow. "Companionship?"

Claire cleared her throat. "We like to share."

Now Kat was thoroughly confused. Share what?

Ronnie's hand found Kat's, and she wrapped her warm fingers around the whole of Kat's hand. Once again, the touch was electrifying, and Kat shivered.

Ronnie winked. "Come and try the bed."

Kat's heart rate leaped, but she seemed powerless as Ronnie led her over to the sumptuous bed.

"Sit." Ronnie tugged Kat nearer the bed. "See how it feels."

Kat did as she was told.

Oh. My. God. This bed is heaven.

"Wow." She spread her arms wide and leaned back slightly, letting her body weight sink into a mattress that seemed more than ready to receive her.

Claire chuckled, and Kat saw the two women exchange a glance. "You like?" Claire asked.

"Uh-huh." Somehow the power of speech had departed, and monosyllabic phrases were all she was capable of.

Ronnie sat next to her to her left. Moments later, Claire sat to Kat's right. They were close. So close. Inhaling the mix of their scents did strange but wonderful things to Kat's entire body. Never mind what the brief press of their legs against hers did. Her nipples hardened by the second, and her clit... Oh God, she was throbbing. She needed to move, to stand up, to get away from the lush sexuality both women represented before she made a complete ass of herself. As soon as she tried to, a hand from each of them, placed slowly but firmly on each of her thighs, prevented her.

"Are you okay, Kat?" Ronnie murmured, her mouth close to Kat's left ear.

"I-I'm not sure." She kept her gaze straight ahead, not daring to look at either of them in case her arousal was plain to see.

Ronnie pulled back and placed a finger on Kat's chin to ease her around to face her. "You find us attractive, yes?"

"What?"

Ronnie simply looked at her, an enigmatic smile on her face.

Oh shit, she doesn't seriously expect me to answer that, does she? Kat looked at Claire and saw the same expectant look on her face, the same mysterious smile.

Oh shit.

May as well just tell it like it is. "Um. Well, yeah. I mean, come on, who wouldn't? Look at you two. I'd have to be dead not to find you attractive."

"We spotted you months ago. Watching us. And we watched you. You're a beautiful woman, Kat." Claire stroked one fingertip along Kat's jawline.

Kat blushed and involuntarily leaned into that touch. "You watched me too?"

She was incredulous. All this time, she'd been gazing at them from afar, and unbeknownst to her, the attraction had been reciprocated. Not that she would have done anything about it, even if she had known—she was way too into Paul to have strayed. But now, free as she was, knowing what she knew now, surrounded by the warmth of the two women, her mind couldn't help but go places where that attraction was acted on.

"Oh yes," Claire said.

Goose bumps broke out over every inch of Kat's skin. Suddenly, her clothes felt too tight, too hot.

"But you never approached, so we assumed you were off-limits somehow and respected whatever that was by not approaching you in return. However much we wanted to." Claire's voice was husky, lower than it had been down in the kitchen.

"Imagine our surprise and joy when we discovered it was you who had answered our ad. Quite the delicious coincidence." Ronnie winked again, and Kat unravelled even further. What were they getting at? Were they suggesting what she thought they were suggesting? When they said share, did they mean—?

"The offer of the room is still on the table, of course," Claire said, her hand now stroking up and down the area of Kat's thigh that was covered by her stockings, between her knee and her hemline. The throbbing in Kat's clit increased in tempo. "And what we are about to offer in addition doesn't affect the room rental at all."

"So if you decline, the room is still yours if you want it," Ronnie said firmly. "There would be no hard feelings, and we wouldn't bring the matter up again."

"Wh-what matter?" She knew she sounded dumb or at least incredibly slow on the uptake, but she needed it spelled out. Said out loud. Because if they were saying what she thought they were saying, she wasn't going to say no. Not with Claire's hand maintaining its perfect rhythm on her thigh, Ronnie's warm breath soft in her ear, and her clit pounding so hard she thought she might come without either of these two women doing anything more than they already were. The evening had turned into something she would never have dreamed of, but she needed to be absolutely certain of what was being offered.

"We would like you to share our bed." Claire said it so matter-of-factly Kat nearly burst out laughing.

"Either for just one night or perhaps for something more long-term." Ronnie's voice was a seductive caress close to Kat's ear.

"Polyamory, you mean?"

Claire shrugged. "It's something we've been discussing."

Kat blinked a few times. "I-I'm not sure about long-term." Her voice was low as she took her time gathering her thoughts. "I've never considered that as an option."

"And that's perfectly okay. We won't push. We are merely offering. If you want to try and it doesn't suit you—or us—then that's fine. Nothing is being forced here at all." It was the most caring Claire had sounded so far, her tone soothing and friendly. "But Kat," she said, leaning closer, her hand stilling its motion for a moment, "we have been attracted to you for quite some time now. We would love to spend some time appreciating you, even if it is just for one night."

"We really would." Ronnie's hand also rubbed sensuous circles on Kat's left thigh.

Kat moaned at the touch. Her mind filtered out all thoughts except where she'd like Ronnie's hand to go next. And then Claire's. She had no idea about the polyamory and shelved that whole concept for now. But a one-night stand, here and now, with these two incredible women? As unbelievable as it sounded to her that the delectable Claire and Ronnie wanted *her*, little Kat, she'd be an idiot to pass up this opportunity.

Her living arrangements completely forgotten, she let her aroused body rule the moment.

"I think I'd like to be appreciated by you." She smiled coyly at Ronnie, then Claire. "I think I'd like that a lot."

Ronnie smiled, her eyes narrowing slightly, and Claire let out an extended "yes" in a hiss. Both women leaned in, their free hands moving swiftly to Kat's back as the hands on her thighs, in unison, slowly dipped under her skirt. When Ronnie's lips nuzzled just below her left ear and Claire's tongue rimmed her right ear, a flood of wetness gushed into Kat's underwear, and she lifted her hips.

"Kiss Claire," Ronnie whispered.

Kat looked at her and saw a gleam in her eyes that sent an exquisite shiver down her back. Smiling, understanding in that moment that a big part of this setup, whatever it turned out to be, was obviously Ronnie's voyeurism, Kat faced Claire. Her lips were already slightly parted, her eyes hooded, and the need on her face made Kat feel powerful. She didn't hesitate any longer. Leaning forward, she took Claire's mouth in a fierce kiss, the kind of kiss she had never let herself fantasise about whenever she'd seen Claire in a club but which she knew, deep down, she'd always wanted to share with her. Her tongue swept into Claire's mouth, emboldened by Claire's soft whimpers. She claimed that mouth, pressing closer, thrilled at the clench of Ronnie's hand on her thigh. Ronnie's breathing was heavy, her arousal clear in the way her body thrust rhythmically against Kat's back as Kat possessed Claire's mouth.

Claire kissed Kat back with as much fervour as she received, but Kat reluctantly broke their connection to suck in air.

"More." Claire's hands moved to Kat's hips and pulled her back.

Kat chuckled but obliged, sinking her tongue deep into Claire's mouth. Ronnie's hands moved as her arms wrapped around Kat from behind; her fingers reached for the hem of Kat's skirt and pulled it higher. Kat whimpered—God, she needed those fingers on her clit, in her pussy, everywhere. She opened her thighs as far as her position enabled, which was frustratingly not far at all. She groaned as Ronnie made the best of it, running her fingers up to the bare skin at the top of Kat's stockings.

"Oh yes," Ronnie said against Kat's ear. "Stockings. My favourite."

Kat didn't remember why she'd worn stockings this morning—there was some practical reason involving not having washed anything else in a few days—but she was oh so thankful she had now, given the reaction they elicited in Ronnie. Her hands dived even farther up Kat's skirt, yanking up the material so her access was improved. Claire wrenched away from Kat's mouth and looked down, watching her partner's fingers as they travelled up the heat of Kat's thighs.

"Is she hot? Wet?" Claire asked, her breathing ragged, her gaze locked on Ronnie's hands.

"Uh-huh." Ronnie moved one finger so it pressed against Kat's pussy, through the silky material of her underwear. Kat's groan was long and low. "So hot. So wet." Ronnie stroked gently, driving Kat mad with the teasing nature of the touch.

"Please," Kat begged, with no shame for doing so.

"Please what?" It was Claire asking, as Ronnie paused her movement, which drove Kat even more insane with want.

"Touch me. Fuck me. Something."

"Mm, what do you think, Ronnie? Shall we?"

Kat tried to grind her pussy against Ronnie's fingertip, but Ronnie chuckled and moved her fingers back just out of reach.

"I think we should," Ronnie said. "But first I want her naked, yes?"

Claire nodded and smiled. "Oh yes, I think naked would be perfect."

They both released Kat, Ronnie pulling her hands back from underneath Kat's skirt, Claire dropping her arms. Kat missed the warmth and the closeness immediately, with something akin to physical pain at their absence.

"Stand up," Claire said, and Kat obeyed. "Strip. Please." Claire smirked on the last word, and the wickedness of it, of what it portended, made Kat's body flush from head to toe.

Adjusting her position so she faced the two women who lounged rather indolently on the bed before her, Kat fumbled to pull her shirt out from her skirt and to undo its buttons.

"Slow down," Ronnie said. "We've got all night."

Kat laughed, a soft snort of a laugh. "You get me this hot and then tell me to go slow?" She shook her head. "Not possible."

Claire's chuckle was throaty. "Mm, I love how eager she is."

Kat finally had the buttons undone and peeled the shirt off her shoulders, revealing the blue plunge bra that held her breasts snuggled in its cups. Kat was not lacking in the breast department and was pleased when Claire and Ronnie murmured simultaneously, "Oh yes," at the sight of Kat's chest.

"Bra off. Now." Claire's eyes narrowed as her face flushed.

Kat obeyed, dropping it to the floor to join the shirt. Free, her breasts hung heavily against her body, her rosy pink nipples rock hard, as they had been since she'd first sat on the bed.

"Fuck me." Ronnie's eyes were wide and her expression hungry.

Claire nodded. "Uh-huh."

Boldly, Kat stepped forward and cupped a breast in each hand, offering up their abundance. The two women before her lunged in, and two hot, wet mouths covered Kat's nipples, pulling and sucking and tugging with teeth and lips. It was intense; her nipples were her most sensitive area, and having them both worked at the same time with equal attention was possibly the most exquisite sensation she'd ever experienced. She looked down, watching her two worshippers, getting just as turned on from watching two women at her breasts as from what they were actually doing. She groaned, her pussy aching for equal attention, but she didn't want to interrupt their current activity.

Ronnie's hands were on the move again, even as she kissed her way around the expanse of Kat's right breast. She reached the zipper at the back of Kat's skirt and pulled it down. Claire must have picked up on what her partner was doing because her hands joined in with the rapid yanking down of Kat's skirt, which pooled at her ankles.

Kat smelled her own scent, heavy in the air between them. Ronnie placed her hands on the sides of Kat's G-string, running her thumbs under the thin piece of material where it hugged Kat's hips.

"Oh God," Kat said as those thumbs swept down, inside the silk, along her pelvis and down to the neatly shaved bush that barely covered her pussy. Ronnie stopped before her thumbs reached Kat's clit, and Kat wanted to howl with frustration.

"Take them off," Claire said to Ronnie, her eyes so dark they were like onyx.

Ronnie did as she was told, pulling the skimpy underwear over the suspender belt and down over the stockings. Evidence of Kat's arousal coated the inside of the material, and Ronnie chuckled as Kat blushed.

"Beautiful," Ronnie said.

"On your back." Claire stared up at Kat but paused to pinch Kat's left nipple between her long fingers, the sharpness of it tugging at Kat's clit. She was even wetter now, felt it flowing everywhere between her legs. When Claire released her nipple with a long, last tug, Kat stepped out of the mess of clothes at her feet and crawled as seductively as she could manage on to the bed through the small open space between Claire and Ronnie. She'd only made it halfway and was still on her hands and knees when Claire's sharp voice said, "Stop."

She stopped. And waited. She was pretty sure they were looking at her, looking at her exposed pussy from behind, her ass framed by the straps of the suspender belt. She felt hands on the backs of her thighs but had no idea whose they were or even how many. The sensations they engendered rolled into one continuous area of arousal as they stroked up and down, side to side, inching ever nearer to her aching pussy.

She groaned as a finger touched her labia, running through the wetness that coated them, smearing it over and over her whole pussy and down the inside of her thighs.

"So wet," Claire said.

"I want to taste," Ronnie said, and Claire groaned in unison with Kat.

"I have an idea." Claire's voice was husky and only just discernible, it was pitched so low. There was a silence then, and Kat tried to peek between her own legs to see what they were doing. All she could see were a few indecipherable hand movements. Then Claire said, "Let her get on her back."

"Okay." Ronnie gently slapped Kat's ass. "You heard the woman. Lay down, please."

Kat giggled and moved forward again until she had inched past them and could turn and lay down. She had no idea what they planned, but whatever it was, she was all for it.

Ronnie met her eyes and winked. "Spread your legs, darling."

As she did so, Claire moved to the end of the bed, grabbed Kat's ankles, and pulled her down the bed a couple of feet. It left her positioned so her pussy was near the foot of the bed, her legs able to hang over the edge with her feet braced on the frame. She was entirely open and exposed, and she watched as Claire drank in the view.

"Perfect," Claire whispered, but Kat didn't know if she meant the position or the view. Or both.

Rustling to her left dragged her attention to Ronnie, and her breath caught in her throat. Ronnie undressed, her baggy jersey dress slinking down her body to reveal a lithe form with small breasts and narrow hips. And lots of muscle. She was tone personified, every movement highlighting beautiful shapes and shadows in her musculature in the soft light of the room.

Kat stared. "You're gorgeous."

"Why, thank you." Ronnie grinned and blew Kat a kiss.

More rustling from her right told her Claire was undressing too. Kat wasn't sure she was ready for this—it was Claire she'd been crushing on all this time, and now she was going to see her in all her glory. Eventually, she turned to look, knowing she couldn't not do so. Her breath hitched. God, she was as gorgeous as Kat had dared imagine. Her breasts were bigger than Ronnie's but not as large as her own. They looked firm, and the dark nipples were huge and hard, and Kat wanted them in her mouth. Claire's body was more curvaceous than Ronnie's and not nearly as toned but beautiful just the same. Her pussy was as shaven as Kat's own, and her clit was prominent, making Kat's mouth water with the thought of sucking on it.

Kat turned her head from left to right, not knowing which woman to look at more and wondering just how long they'd leave her lying here between them, her legs wide open, before one or both of them did something about the fact that they were all naked and turned on.

"Ready?" Claire asked Ronnie across Kat's body. Ronnie was flicking her gaze between Kat's flat stomach, her strong thighs, and her breasts, which she was clearly a fan of, if her hungry expression was anything to go by.

"Hell, yes."

Kat didn't have to wait much longer to find out what they had planned. In a perfectly synchronised action, Ronnie moved to the foot of the bed and knelt before Kat's opened legs, which made her moan with anticipation, while Claire climbed onto the bed beside Kat and rearranged Kat's arms so they were in line with her own body. Then she straddled Kat's head, and Kat nearly forgot to breathe.

"Lick me good, Kat," Claire said from above her, her eyes staring down at Kat with a delicious intensity.

Kat nodded and opened her mouth, her arms lifting so her palms could brace against Claire's lush hips. Just as Claire lowered herself onto Kat's waiting tongue, the exquisite sensation of Ronnie's tongue dragging through Kat's wet pussy assaulted her senses. She let out a cry of ecstasy that was muffled by Claire's wet pussy covering her mouth and chin.

Oh God, I have actually died and gone to heaven.

It was hard to focus. Ronnie's tongue was like silk against her pussy, while Claire's wet and musky pussy slid over Kat's tongue and lips as she ground down against Kat. If Kat focused on her own pleasure, she almost forgot to move her tongue to meet Claire's needs—and yet, if she focused on Claire's desires, she lost some of the connection with the sensations Ronnie elicited from her own body. She concentrated, working hard to find a balance point where both things were possible, and when she found it, she whimpered with the intensity of the feelings. Claire rode her face now, using her just how she needed her, whispering words Kat couldn't decipher interspersed with cries of "Oh God, just there, *right* there." Her thighs clenched and unclenched against Kat's head, and Kat's own legs pumped harder the more Ronnie pressed her tongue and mouth against Kat's pussy. Ronnie's hands held onto Kat's hips, keeping her pinned to the bed while she dived inside Kat with her tongue, pushing deep and working in and out, slowly fucking Kat, making Kat's thighs quake with the sensations.

"Harder, Kat." Claire's voice was ragged, as if she was close to coming undone, and that turned Kat on even more.

She moaned against Claire's pussy as she licked her harder. Kat wanted to focus on Claire now, wanted to make her come, feel her break apart all over Kat's face. Her own orgasm could wait; she knew Ronnie wouldn't mind. She flicked her tongue slightly higher on Claire's clit, and the gasps and groans that came from above her told her she made the right move. She opened her eyes wide to take in the sight of Claire in ecstasy above her. It was a glorious sight—Claire's hair, normally so perfectly maintained, was wild and bedraggled, bouncing on her shoulders as she pumped her hips against Kat's face. Her eyes were closed, her lips parted as she huffed out her breath in ragged chops. Her breasts hung a little low as she bent forward, and Kat wished she could reach them. Maybe next time. Because, oh God, there had to be a next time. Once was not enough, nowhere near.

"Oh fuck!" With one last huge thrust of her hips, Claire cried out, arching her back and slamming her hands against the mattress as her orgasm took over. She coated Kat's mouth with a small gush of fluid, and Kat lapped it up, already wondering when she'd be allowed to do this again because this, unravelling the apparently unflappable Claire, was addictive.

Before she could linger on that thought, however, Ronnie upped her game, and all Kat could think about was the immense pleasure coursing through her own clit. She pulled her head away from Claire's pussy to gasp aloud as Ronnie sucked her clit between her lips, French-kissing it with a slow seductiveness that made Kat's toes curl.

"Oh God," Kat whispered.

Ronnie moaned against her before lifting her head. "You like that, Kat?"

"Fuck, *yes*." Kat gripped Claire's hips tighter, her fingers digging into the pliant flesh, breathing in the scent of Claire, who now stroked Kat's hair.

"I want to hear you," Claire said, pushing a finger between Kat's lips and out again, fucking her mouth and eliciting a groan from deep in Kat's throat. "I want to hear how good Ronnie makes you feel. I want to hear you come all over Ronnie's face." She withdrew her finger and rocked back slightly. Kat just about managed to open her eyes against the onslaught of sensation Ronnie gave her, and she locked gazes with Claire. "Tell me. Tell me what she's doing to you," Claire said.

"Fuck, her...her tongue is amazing," Kat said. "She's...she's licking me *so* hard." It was difficult to talk, but it turned her on, so she kept going. "I'm so close. God, Ronnie, fuck me at the same time, *please*."

Claire groaned and twisted her head around to watch as Ronnie slid one finger deep into Kat's pussy. Kat bucked and gasped, desperate to be filled.

"More," she cried. "More."

Ronnie obliged with a second finger, then a third. She owned Kat with those long fingers, pushing ever deeper inside her while her tongue still worked wonders on Kat's clit.

"That's it," Claire said, her voice ragged. "Fuck her, baby. Fuck her hard."

"Yes, yes! Fuck me hard." Kat was almost shouting, her legs thrashing, the orgasm building so strongly she was afraid it would rip her apart when it finally hit. Ronnie fucked her harder and faster, worked her tongue harder and faster, and that was it. Kat spiralled over the edge and disappeared into a space filled with light and stars and heat and pleasure so intense it was almost painful.

"Fuck, yesssss!" Her hips pushed up so high, her spine creaked. Claire rode her like a bucking horse, her hand gripped into Kat's hair, while Ronnie moaned and lapped at Kat's swollen clit as if she couldn't get enough, didn't want to stop.

Kat flailed an arm in Ronnie's direction without being able to reach her and finally managed to gasp out the words, "Stop, please," before flopping back onto the bed. Ronnie removed her tongue, and Kat whimpered in relief and sorrow. Yes, she'd needed Ronnie to stop, but now that she was gone, Kat's pussy ached with loneliness.

Claire eased off Kat's body and collapsed beside her on top of the duvet, groaning and chuckling as she rubbed her legs. Ronnie stood and climbed over the end of the bed, crawling up the covers to lay half on Claire, half on Kat. All three women moaned at the contact, and arms wrapped around whatever area of whoever's body they could get hold of. They were an entwined mesh of limbs and warm skin and wet pussies. Kat was suffused with contentment, but Ronnie's soft groans broke her reverie.

"You okay?" Claire whispered in Ronnie's direction. "What do you need, babe?"

"You know what I need," Ronnie said hoarsely.

"Oh yeah."

Kat listened and watched and waited for whatever would happen soon, desperately hoping she could be a part of it too. *Although just being a spectator would be pretty hot too.*

Suddenly, there was movement. Ronnie wriggled off Claire to lay entirely on top of Kat and smiled down at her as their mouths came close. Then she kissed Kat, the first time their lips had met since the evening's festivities had begun. Kat tasted herself on Ronnie's full lips, and it sent sparks of desire shooting through her pussy yet again. Ronnie's mouth was bigger than Claire's, covering Kat's entirely as she sucked Kat's tongue deep into her mouth.

Claire rolled off the bed, and Kat heard rummaging in a drawer somewhere.

"That's it, babe," Claire said huskily. "Enjoy her. Suck her nipples."

Ronnie did as instructed and moved downwards to Kat's breasts. Kat wasn't sure if she could stand any more stimulation, but that thought fled as Ronnie's hot mouth took one of her nipples in and laved it with her tongue. It was wondrous how quickly Kat's pussy could respond again after the enormous orgasm only minutes before.

"Fuck, that looks so hot." Claire was still doing something to Kat's right, but she had no idea what until she heard the chink of buckles and a sharp intake of breath from Ronnie. Forcing her eyes open and turning her head, Kat's brain nearly short-circuited as she took in the sight of Claire in a black leather harness with a blue dildo, some eight inches in length, jutting out from between her legs.

"Holy crap," Kat whispered. "*That* is fucking hot."

Ronnie let go of Kat's nipple with a wet pop and turned to look at Claire. Kat couldn't see her reaction, only hear it. The groan was long and tortured, and before it ended, Ronnie lifted her body away from Kat's, moving to the centre of the bed and placing herself on all fours. Kat scrambled out of the way as Claire knelt on the edge of the bed.

"No, don't move away too far. You're going to play a part in this too." Claire grabbed Kat's arm. "I'm going to fuck her just the way she likes it, but you're going to make her come."

Kat inhaled and nearly choked. Even watching this would be beyond arousing, never mind taking part. She shifted on the bed so she had a perfect view of Ronnie's soaking wet pussy awaiting Claire's cock.

Ronnie moaned. "Claire, are you going to make me wait even longer?"

"Shush." Claire moved into position behind Ronnie's ass, which she held high in the air, her forearms bracing her against the mattress. "You'll get what you need, babe, don't you worry." And without a moment's hesitation, she slid into Ronnie's pussy in one smooth motion. Ronnie howled with pleasure, and her fists thumped against the bed as she ground her hips backwards, taking in more of the dildo until it was sunk inside her up to its hilt.

"Oh my God," Kat whispered, hugely turned on again at the show.

Claire fucked her partner, each thrust eliciting another tortured moan from Ronnie. Claire's hands, which had been on Ronnie's hips, released their hold a tad. In the next moment, Kat knew why—as Claire pulled back, revealing more of Ronnie's perfectly toned ass, she delivered a sharp slap to Ronnie's right buttock.

"Yes!" Ronnie's voice rang out in the otherwise quiet room. Kat's clit throbbed in response.

Claire drove into Ronnie again, then out again and on the outstroke, delivered another stinging slap to Ronnie's ass.

"Yes. Oh God, baby, so good. Don't stop." Ronnie's voice sounded one step away from a sob.

Kat was torn between watching the dildo pump in and out of her glistening pussy, gazing at Ronnie's pert breasts as they bounced with each movement, or staring at Ronnie's face as her ecstasy played out in exquisite relief.

"Kat," Claire said sharply, "Ronnie needs you."

Kat blinked a few times and dragged her gaze away from Ronnie's body to stare at Claire. "She does?"

"Oh yes." Claire drove into Ronnie once more. "She needs to come soon."

"Uh-huh?" Kat was back to being dumb with arousal, and she was amazed Claire was being so patient with her.

"You can use your mouth or your fingers, whatever's easiest. Normally, she gets herself off when I fuck her like this, but tonight you can have the pleasure. I think Ronnie would like that."

Ronnie grunted her agreement as Claire continued to fuck her hard, both of them panting with the exertion, the soft sheen of perspiration on their bodies glinting in the low light.

Kat surveyed the scene. While it would be technically possible to get her head underneath Ronnie and manoeuvre to where she could lick her clit, by far the easiest option would be to use her fingers. And, of course, if she did that, she could still watch the fucking show at the same time. Decision made.

She shimmied down the bed a little and pressed herself against the side of Ronnie's hip. From here, she had the perfect view of Claire's cock as it slipped so easily in and out of Ronnie's soaking wet pussy, but she should also have an easy reach to Ronnie's clit. She slipped her hand around Ronnie's flat stomach and down through the tight curls at the apex of her thighs. Ronnie moaned, a strangled sound that cut off in a long gasp as Claire smacked her ass again.

"Please," Ronnie said. "Please…"

Kat found Ronnie's clit—it was hard and swollen and sitting high and proud between her labia, which had spread wide to accommodate the girth of the dildo Claire wielded. Kat placed two fingers on either side of the clit and rubbed, slowly and gently at first, but with Ronnie's moans increasing as she did so, upping the pressure and the tempo.

"Yes, oh yes." Ronnie threw her hips back, both to take in more of the dildo and to grind herself against Kat's fingers. Kat read the signs, heard Ronnie's sounds rising in volume, and knew she was close. Without breaking her rhythm, she moved her fingers so they pressed down fully on Ronnie's clit. Claire thrust deeper, Kat rubbed harder, and moments later, Ronnie bucked and wailed and came, gushing over the dildo and Kat's fingers. Her cry was loud and long, her pelvis pushed far back into Claire's groin. Claire stopped moving, keeping herself buried deep within her lover, and Kat stilled her fingers, keeping pressure with no movement. She glanced up at Claire. She was dishevelled again, but she smiled at Kat and beckoned her near. They kissed, long and deep, the three-way connection between them and Ronnie maintained like a strand of DNA, with Claire still deep inside her and Kat still holding firmly to her clit.

Ronnie reached back and gently pushed Claire's hip. Claire eased out of Ronnie before sitting back on her heels. Ronnie's hand then moved to Kat's, pressing her once more into her clit before lifting her hand away from her swollen flesh. When she had done so, Ronnie collapsed facedown on the bed. A moment later, a loud burst of laughter escaped her lips.

Claire chuckled, and Kat giggled, and soon the three of them guffawed. By some unspoken agreement, Claire and Kat flopped onto the bed on either side of Ronnie and wrapped an arm each over her body. She turned to each of them, Claire first, then Kat, and kissed them slowly. There was a tenderness there, and it flipped Kat's stomach in a decidedly pleasant way. They lay like that for some minutes, their breathing gradually easing back to a normal rhythm, the scent of delicious sex hanging in the air around them.

What now? Kat wondered briefly, but as soon as her mind formed the question, she knew the answer. Nel would think she was mad, but Kat didn't care. This felt extraordinarily right.

Rolling onto her side so she could see both Claire and Ronnie and waiting until they looked directly at her, she smiled. "So when did you say I could move in?"

It's Getting Hot in Here

Alison Grey

Linda wiped her sweaty palms on her silk pajama pants. It was kind of ridiculous how nervous she was. The phone lay beside her, and she kept staring at it as if it were the forbidden fruit in the Garden of Eden.

She took a deep breath to calm down just as the phone rang. *Showtime!* She pressed the button to accept the call. "Hello," she murmured in a hopefully sexy way into the receiver.

"Hi." The low female voice on the other end made Linda shiver. "What's your name?"

Linda paused. *Dammit.* She should have made up a name beforehand. "Uh, Candy." She winced at her stupid choice.

"Candy?" Soft chuckling drifted through the line. "Sounds…sweet."

Linda giggled before she could stop it. "Well, yeah."

"This is your first time, isn't it?"

"Uh-huh."

"Don't worry. I'll take good care of you."

The words sent a shiver through her body. But wait. Wasn't she supposed to be the one to take care of the caller? Linda cleared her throat. "So what do you want me to do?"

An audible gulp sounded. "Let's start with telling me where you are."

"I'm lying on my bed."

"Are the lights on?"

"Yes. The lamp on the bedside table."

"Turn it off. I want you to only feel, not see."

Her mouth went dry. "I can do that." She turned off the light. "Okay. It's dark."

"Good. Tell me what you're wearing."

"White silk pajamas." Oh, that might not be considered very sexy. "They're incredibly soft, and I'm just moving my hand over the fabric. It's cool to the touch but feels very sensual." Ugh. Even for a first timer, that was bad.

"Sounds like it. So, Candy, why don't you move your fingers over the fabric from your belly to one of your breasts?"

Linda sucked in a breath. She liked where this was going. "Oh yeah. My hand is sliding up…and up. Now I'm lightly stroking my breast." She bit her lip when her nipple hardened and tingling spread from it, even though it was only a hint of a touch. "And now?"

"Knead your breast slowly. Not hard. Just…right."

"Mmh, feels good. What now?"

The breathing on the other line hitched. "Roll your nipple between your fingers. Through the silk."

Linda obeyed. Pleasure surged through her from her nipple straight to her clit. She exhaled loudly.

"Are you holding the phone?"

"Yes."

"Put me on speakerphone. I want you to use both hands."

Oh yeah! Linda pressed the button for it and placed the phone on the bedside table. "Both of my hands are free now. Tell me what you want."

Ragged breathing filtered through the line. "Oh, I will. Use your left hand to pleasure your other breast."

Impatient, Linda brought her left hand to her other breast. "O-okay. Yeah. Feels good."

"I bet it does. Keep doing it, and move your right hand down your body. Slowly."

Her fingertips drifted across the soft silk. The sensual brush made her shiver.

"Don't go too far. Stay out of your pants. But…"

"But what?" Linda asked, eager to continue.

"Touch yourself through the material."

Quickly, her free hand moved past her belly, leaving a prickling in its wake. She spread her legs and, a second later, grasped her center, hot even through the silk of the pajama pants and her panties. Her core throbbed. A groan escaped her lips. She wanted more. Now.

"Don't you dare move your hand down there. Just hold."

Oh God. She couldn't be serious. "Maybe a little bit?"

"No."

Linda took a calming breath and forced herself to ignore the pulsing of her most intimate place. "Whatever you want me to do. I'm yours."

"Yes. You are."

"What about you?" Linda tried hard to ignore the almost painful thudding of her intimate parts. "What are you weari—?"

"Doesn't matter."

She wanted to complain but didn't have the chance when the next command came. "Now, move your palm between your legs. Slowly. Very slowly."

It was torture, but Linda surrendered. Dampness spread under her hand, and a pleasant tingle expanded through her body.

"Not too fast. We have all the time in the world."

Suppressing a curse, Linda slowed her movement.

"Oh yeah. Just like that." The voice on the other end sounded rougher. "Now squeeze your breast a little more."

Heat spread from her breast at the careful touch of her warm hand.

"More."

Linda's eyes fell shut. The temperature in the room seemed to skyrocket. How was it possible to be so aroused, especially fully clothed?

"Let's get back to your other hand, shall we?"

Linda nodded eagerly, even though she couldn't be seen.

"Use more pressure with your palm."

Instead of answering, Linda moaned at the delicious feeling of her quickening motion causing her clit to twitch in the most delightful way possible. Her breathing became faster too.

"Hey." There was a smirk in the caller's voice. "Is someone eager to speed things up?"

"Yeah. Please. Can I—?"

"No. Not so fast, tiger. Let's get you out of your clothes first."

Clumsy with need, Linda shed her top, pants, and drenched panties in record time and covered herself with a thin sheet. "Okay." She was breathless from struggling out of her clothes and from arousal.

Laughter reverberated through the line. It sounded as if coming from an angel. "I was about to tell you to take off your top, but I have a feeling you couldn't wait and got ahead of things, huh?"

Linda's cheeks warmed, and it had nothing to do with the arousal she felt. "Sorry."

"God, you're adorable." Rustling followed by a muffled "ugh" could be heard. "We're both naked now."

"Where are your hands?" Linda asked.

The clicking of a tongue came through the phone. "Nice try. But you know enough. From now on, do exactly as I say, understand?"

Linda had never been into any form of submission and certainly not in the bedroom. But the commanding voice did things to her that made it hard to form any coherent thought. All her nerve endings seemed at attention and ready to turn the sizzling flowing through her body into a firework. "I promise."

"Good. So, first of all, don't even think about touching yourself there again before I tell you."

Dammit! Reluctant, Linda moved her hand back to her belly but couldn't resist sliding her hand along the way, the caress causing a million tiny sparks between her legs. A sigh escaped her before she could stop it. "Okay. What now?"

"Not so eager. I want to take my time with you."

Linda frowned. What if she wanted to speed things up? Maybe if she… "Where are your hands?"

"What did I say earlier? We're talking about you…Candy. Take both of your breasts into your hands. And knead. Not too soft. Be rough."

She wasn't one for rough, and it wasn't really painful, but when she massaged her sensitive breasts and squeezed a little bit more than she usually liked, lightning seemed to blast to her core. Her eyelids became heavy.

"Tell me how it feels."

"Good." Linda grunted. "So damn good. Turns me on."

Loud panting was the only answer.

"What now?" Linda asked. "What do you want me to do?"

"M-move your right hand to the inside of your thigh. Start just above the knee. Move it up one side, then the other, but don't touch your center."

Linda's hand rushed down and caressed the inside of her right leg, then her left. The sensual caress was calming and arousing all at once. "Let me touch myself."

"You are touching yourself, honey." The voice sounded much too amused for Linda's liking but at the same time pretty breathless.

"Maybe just a little bi—"

"Move with one finger, only one, to where you want to have it."

Linda gasped when her index finger dove through her drenched folds, rubbing slowly over her clit, sending a thousand tiny lightning bolts of ecstasy there. She couldn't remember ever feeling something like that before.

"Did I tell you to move your finger?"

Linda opened her eyes that had fallen shut without her realizing it and blinked. How had she been found out? "Sorry." She hated that she had to stop moving. It was becoming torture. "Maybe just a little bit?"

"Only if you do it very slowly." There was a smile in the soft voice.

"Ohhh." Linda circled her nub, applying just the right amount of pressure. Her world narrowed to the rhythmic movement.

"Two fingers."

"Yes!" Linda circled faster. Dizziness overcame her, but she didn't care. The all-consuming heat between her legs was all she could think about.

"Roll your nipple between your fingers."

The friction on her nipple sent a new wave of pleasure through Linda's body.

"Enter yourself with two fingers." The words were more panted than spoken. "Now!"

Gritting her teeth, she forced her fingers away from her throbbing clit and carefully entered herself. Her tight inner walls clamped around her fingers, and a nearly overwhelming surge of arousal flooded her body.

"Use your thumb on your clit. Listen to my rhythm. In, out, in, out, yeah."

Linda rubbed herself frantically, rougher than she usually would. The building tension deep in her belly made her whimper.

Panting drifted through the line. "Just like that. Or maybe…a little bit faster. No, much faster." Loud moaning. "Harder. Push inside. Push, push, push."

Linda pumped her fingers deep inside. She was so wet, but because she was so close already, she was tight, and the friction caused by that drove her crazy.

"Use a third finger."

She was well past speaking but obeyed. Her eyes squeezed shut when her orgasm started to build. "I'm coming!" It crashed over her. "Ahhh!" She arched against her hand one last time before falling back onto the soft mattress. Her heart raced, and she struggled to get enough air into her lungs. "Wow," she croaked when she could finally speak again.

A second later, a long sigh vibrated through the phone, and Linda couldn't suppress a smile. She obviously wasn't the only one who had come.

"Where are your fingers?" The question was more breathed than spoken.

Linda grinned. "Still inside." She was about to withdraw them when she was told not to. "Uh, but—"

"No. Leave them inside. Don't move them. Stroke your clit gently. Only a hint of a touch."

Skeptical that she could come a second time by her own hand in such quick succession, she barely brushed the sensitive nub and almost jumped from the bed. "It's sensitive."

"I bet it is." Again the words were more breathed than spoken. It was incredibly sexy. "You have to move very lightly. Caress your clit. Don't rub too hard. Imagine it's my tongue licking it."

Because of all the fast breathing, her mouth was dry already, but now the last bit of fluid was gone as if every drop had moved south. "God, yeah, lick me." Linda's thumb became more insistent, sending sparks once again through her drenched center.

"Slip your fingers out now. Use them all to rub your clit."

Linda withdrew her fingers and shuddered at the sensation. Her fingers felt hot against her wet folds, and when they touched her nub, she couldn't hold back a loud groan.

"Feels good, huh?"

"Yeah," Linda shouted, her movements becoming faster with every stroke.

"Stop!"

Linda blinked. "What?"

"Stop it. Take your fingers away."

"What the—?"

"Get off the bed. Stand up and lean against the wall."

Clenching her teeth to hold back a curse, she let go of her breast she had begun to fondle again and threw back the sheet. Thankfully, the light was out, so nobody would be able to see her through the window. She walked to the wall beside the door, trembling with frustration and arousal. "You really want me to lean against the wall?"

"Yes."

When her overheated skin hit the cold wall, Linda flinched. "Okay. I'm leaning against the wall," she said more loudly so she could be heard even though the phone was still on her bedside table.

"Very good." Her counterpart either didn't notice the irritation in Linda's voice, or she simply ignored it. "Imagine that I'm pressing you against the wall and it's my fingers now that touch you."

Linda hissed when the fingers of her right hand found her clit. The short walk through the room had taken enough time to cool her dripping, wet fingers. It was surprisingly arousing. She resumed her rhythm. Her fingers warmed within a few strokes, but the cold wallpaper pressing against her back didn't. It felt wild and wonderful.

"Don't be shy. Show me how fast you can come. Let me hear how it feels when you grind your fingers against your clit. Hard."

"Oh God!" Linda rubbed her fingers roughly against her clit, the friction driving her crazy. Her legs felt like rubber, so she pressed even more against the cool wall, using it as support.

"Come for me." The whispered command was the most erotic thing Linda had ever heard.

"Holy shit!" Bright spots flashed in front of her eyes when the orgasm crashed over her. She sank to the floor, no longer able to stand.

Silence filtered through the line, then a soft, "Are you okay?"

Linda gulped a few mouthfuls of air. "Fine." She stood on wobbly legs, stumbled back to the bed, and slipped beneath the sheets. "H-how about you?"

Snickering. "Never been better."

A fond smile formed on Linda's lips. "I miss you."

"I miss you too, my love."

"Christina?"

"Mmh?"

"Why haven't we ever made love against a wall?"

Christina's laughter warmed Linda's heart. "Good question. Guess we'll have to do that when I'm back."

Linda grinned. "Definitely. And also the shower."

"Oh my God. I created a sex monster."

"That you did."

"So," Christina said in a singsong voice, "how did you like your first phone sex conversation?"

Linda's body still buzzed. "It was incredible. Makes me wonder why I didn't go through with it when I called your phone sex hotline back then. Anyway, thanks for talking me into it. I can see why your former customers liked it so much."

"It was nothing like that with them." Christina's playful voice became serious.

Stupid, stupid, stupid. Linda had come to terms with Christina's former job at a sex hotline a while back, but from time to time, especially when she tried to be casual about Christina's past, she often failed miserably. "I'm sorry. I didn't mean to—"

"No, it's fine. I know how you meant it." Christina sighed. "I'm glad you liked it. I liked it too. Very much so." A smile had returned to her voice.

"Did you come too?"

"Yeah." Christina chuckled. "Twice."

"Are you in bed?"

"Oh no. We're not going to do it again. Seriously, Linda. I'm beat."

Torn between disappointment and relief, because her body was spent as well, Linda rolled onto her side and snuggled into her pillow. "It was a long day, huh?"

"It was, but there are only three days left, then I'll finally be free."

After quitting her job at the sex hotline, Christina had worked at a building cleaning company. The work was physically challenging, but at least her working hours were flexible enough to allow her to get her secondary school diploma. And while they now lived more than three hundred miles apart, next week Christina would move in with her and put an end to their many months of a long-distance relationship. It was a dream come true. For more than a year, they had essentially seen each other only on the weekends. Now with Christina moving from Cologne to Berlin, nothing would ever separate them again. And because Christina would begin her study of architecture at the TU Berlin, Linda also didn't have to worry about work separating them anytime soon.

"And how was your day?" Christina asked after a few moments of silence.

"Oh, the usual. Well, one patient brought his mouse to our session."

"Did you say mouse?"

"Yeah. He has a mouse as a pet. And, uh, he's pretty attached to it. Anyway, I asked him not to bring the mouse again."

Christina giggled. "I think I would have screamed if someone suddenly took a mouse out of his bag."

"Actually, it crawled out of his collar. He must have had the mouse under his shirt the whole time on the way over. I nearly had a heart attack because I didn't expect something like that."

"Who would? Oh God." Christina hesitated. "That isn't healthy, right? I mean, your patient. Is he—?"

"You know I can't tell you more." As a psychologist, she had to keep her patients' information confidential.

"You're right. I'm sorry."

"No, it's fine." Linda had her practice in an extra room in her apartment. That had never been an issue, but now that Christina would move in with her, Linda would have to rent an office space to avoid Christina meeting her patients. Without a doubt, it would be good for Linda too.

"What are you thinking?" Christina asked when Linda didn't say anything for a while.

"Oh, I just thought that me getting an extra office will be good for both of us. I mean, before we met, all I had was my work, so, of course, I worked from home."

"You have gotten so much better, though."

"Yeah. Because of you." Linda smiled. Another person could never be solely responsible for your happiness, but Christina had opened a door for her. A door to a life worth living. Together. "Everything has changed."

"For the better?" The insecurity in Christina's voice made Linda's heart ache.

"Definitely." It was time to lighten the mood again. "And I don't only say that because I just came two times."

Christina snorted. "I hope not. Although…"

"Although what?"

It took a few moments for Christina to answer, as if she wasn't sure if she should voice her thoughts. "Wanna make it three times?" Her voice had dropped a register.

"What do you…? Oh."

"Is that a yes?"

Why had Christina changed her mind? Because Linda's therapy sessions didn't begin before nine in the morning, she had a slightly different sleeping rhythm than her beautiful partner. But more often than not, it was Christina who didn't want to end their long evening calls. Earlier though, it had been Christina who had wanted to cut things short. "I thought you're beat. It's almost midnight already, and I know you have to get up at half past five."

"You're right. But—"

"But what?"

Christina blew out a breath. "I'm really tired, but I'm still kind of tense."

"Why, honey? Is it because of my stupid comment?"

"What do you mean? About my former customers?" When Linda confirmed, Christina said, "No. Having phone sex with my girlfriend is nothing like talking with a horny guy for money. Besides, there's a reason I decided that you would be playing the one working for the phone sex line. I never called such a number."

"No, I did." Not that anything sexual had happened between them back then. Linda bit her lip. At least not on the phone.

Both chuckled.

"I'm glad you did," Christina said, "or we would have never met."

"Maybe, maybe not. So want to tell me why you're still tense after coming two times in a row?"

"You will laugh when I tell you."

"Laugh? No. I promise not to. Shoot."

Christina kept silent for a few seconds. "I'm not sure that's it. Ah, it's probably only PMS."

"Christina, tell me."

"Okay, okay." Christina sighed. "I was packing today after my shift. The last three boxes for moving, actually."

"And?" While working as a therapist, Linda was much more patient, but here and now she was really curious and also a little worried what this was all about.

"And I packed up all our dildos."

Linda blinked. And blinked again. "I think you lost me."

"God." Christina's voice sounded muffled, as if she was holding a hand or a sheet in front of her face. Seconds later, her voice was clear again. "I was totally turned on when I remembered you and me using the purple strap-on last month, but when I wanted to…you know…"

Linda knew exactly what Christina meant. A pleasant shudder coursed through her body when she remembered their last time with the strap-on. "Oh, I know."

"Anyway, my mom called just before I, uh, could make use of it."

It was incredible how a seasoned phone sex worker could sound so flustered over a sex toy. It was cute and sweet and so typical Christina. Linda held back a laugh. "I see. So she stopped you from having fun, and I guess afterward you were not in the mood anymore." Her mouth went dry. "Wait, did you use it earlier when we…?"

"No. That's just it. When I look at it now, I think of my mom."

As a psychologist, Linda was used to controlling her emotional reactions, but nothing could have held back the laughter that broke out of her now. "I-I'm sorry." It turned into a howl. "Really."

"You promised not to laugh."

Dammit, she was right. Linda pulled herself together. "Please forgive me."

Christina huffed. "It's fine. I would probably find it funny too if the purple one wasn't my favorite toy. But, jeez, I can't stop thinking about it. Seriously, I've been horny for hours. I thought the phone sex would help. I'm totally beat now, but still…"

"Horny?"

A loud exhale. "Yeah."

Linda rubbed her hand over her face but paused when she smelled herself on her fingers. She told Christina about it.

"God, Linda. I would love to taste you now."

Her body tingled at the thought. "Next week, my love. For now, how about you get the blue dolphin dildo out of the box? Let's forget the purple one."

"The dolphin?"

"Uh-huh."

"Mmh. On one condition. You use the glass dildo at the same time."

Linda jumped out of the bed, not bothering to turn on the light. "Let's get our little friends, and this time I will tell you what to do."

∽∾∾

If you enjoyed this short story, check out Alison Grey's novella *Hot Line*, in which Christina and Linda met and fell in love.

STRESS MANAGEMENT

Lola Keeley

"You're doing too much," Asha says as they enter Regan's apartment, the door shuddering closed behind them. "I know what that looks like. I know what burning the candle at both ends, then setting a whole box of candles on fire for good measure looks like. You crashed the car tonight, but it could have been much worse."

"I thought I had it under control." Regan's shoulders slump. She knows she's lucky to be standing there, unscathed. Taking a turn far too wide on her usual route home had left her Mini spliced by a streetlamp and her very lucky to escape with a few bruises. "I have been pretty tired. Work is crazy, but that's no excuse." She doesn't want pity about her screwups, not from Asha.

"It is if you stop beating yourself up about it." Asha folds her arms, defiant once more. The soft lamplight makes her dark complexion glow, brings out the subtle lines of her arms that have been toned through near religious discipline at the gym. "And start taking better care of yourself. I like dating you, but I can't do that if you burn yourself out."

"I'll book a spa day once this deal is closed. Thanks for coming to pick me up."

Regan tries not to think about how much work will be waiting at her office in the morning. She can't complain, though, as her real estate work is nothing compared to running a whole company as Asha does. Regan grabs water from the fridge that dominates one corner of her modest studio apartment, offering one to her guest, but Asha declines with a shake of her head.

"We both know you're lying." Asha brushes a long strand of black hair from her face. "So I'd like to try something. Do you trust me?"

"Of course I trust you."

Regan puts the bottle down and takes Asha's hands. It's still pleasing how, even in flats, she still has a few inches over Asha, though she feels out of place in her gym clothes while Asha is still office smart, her formfitting dress and heels as immaculate as they must have been that morning.

"So now it's just a case of giving you want you want. Or, more accurately, what you need."

"I don't even know what that is."

Regan sighs. She hasn't pulled the curtains, and only the lamp by the door is on. Her full-length windows send the neon of downtown Los Angeles lights bouncing against the shadows of the space. At least they're higher than the surrounding buildings, too high to be overlooked. Normally, Asha wouldn't be caught dead in this part of town; she has a sprawling place out in the Hollywood Hills that looks like a movie set.

Asha silences her with a kiss, lingering and sweet.

"That's okay, sweetheart," she says. "Just come with me."

Asha leads her into the bedroom until they're standing face-to-face at the foot of the bed. She ducks away to switch on two lamps, bathing the room in a soft glow that makes Regan think of summer evenings and fireflies. The space has never felt like that before.

"First things first, get out of those workout clothes. This isn't a chore or an obligation." Asha watches, still as a statue. "Stop thinking. Just do as I tell you."

"But—"

"If at any point you want to stop, just pick a word that you'll remember. The minute you say that word, we stop. It's exactly that simple, darling."

"I like it when you call me *darling*," Regan says. "Can that be the word?"

"No, because I reserve the right to use it. Something you would never usually say in bed."

"Venus." Regan plucks the planet's name from thin air, but it feels right.

"Good. Now, I believe I told you to get undressed. Strip for me, Regan."

Regan nods, her fingers trembling as she fumbles with the zipper on her hoodie. Instead of coming closer, Asha gives a quiet hum of approval and retreats to the chair that sits to the side of Regan's bed. When Asha takes her seat, it becomes a throne, her delicate wrists resting on the arms of it. She crosses her legs with a hint of Sharon Stone about the gesture.

Asha is Regan's audience, and she's waiting for her show.

Regan shrugs off the hooded jacket and tugs at the hem of her running vest, biting her bottom lip to concentrate on taking her time. Already she feels less overwhelmed, less yelled at by the world around her. Asha's going to tell her what to do. Asha's going to make her feel better. Regan doesn't have to make the plans or think outside the box or deal with any of the problems hurled at her today. It's just this room, Asha, and the hint of a breeze against Regan's skin as she strips to her underwear.

"How cute." Asha tilts her head. "Although the sports-bra-and-boxers look really does work on you."

"I got changed to work out. I have other things in the drawers if—"

Asha cuts her off with a wave of one imperious finger. "No talking. For you. Just your word if you need it."

Regan nods. She can get used to this.

"Now the shoes." Asha frowns at the running shoes in black with neon green detailing. "You can be quick about those."

Regan toes them off and kicks them toward the corner. Asha's gaze rakes her body from head to toe, her eyes predatory. Regan rests her hands on her hips, resisting the urge to take a few steps over there and to climb onto Asha as she so badly wants to.

"Come this way," Asha says after an eternity. As Regan moves closer, Asha shakes her head. "Not to me. Hands on the bed. Bend over."

Regan's breath catches in her throat at the firmness of the command, but she shakes her ass a little as she turns, taking the position as ordered.

She's glad of the focus when Asha leans forward, the gentle air from her words brushing the sensitive skin of Regan's ass as she speaks.

"I'm not going to touch you," she says, and Regan's heart sinks. "Yet." Regan heaves a sigh of relief. "I am going to make sure that you touch yourself," Asha says. "You remember we've talked before about the importance of finding a release?"

Regan nods. She's never done this before with a witness. She has barely admitted to another person that she touches herself ever, but the thought of doing it under Asha's gaze shocks her body with a silent thrill.

"Don't be shy," Asha says, her voice lower and husky now. She sounds like late nights and really expensive Scotch. Each word draws a physical throb in Regan's body. "Get up on the bed now. On your knees and face me."

It shouldn't be hard to follow that instruction, though to Regan's embarrassment, her hand slips for a second, and she has to stop herself from face-planting when she first changes position. She faces Asha. There's no hiding from that gaze. She wants to ask if this is what Asha wants, if Regan is giving her what she's asking for, but the order not to talk sits like an invisible band across her tongue. When Regan parts her lips in an unasked question, Asha smiles.

"Perfect," Asha says. "You're doing so well, darling."

Regan shivers at the endearment, hands hanging at her sides as she kneels in black underwear, dark blonde hair falling around her shoulders with a strand or two already wild across her face. She's aware of every inch of her body, caressed as it is by Asha's gaze. It's almost as good as being touched, but she craves that now more than ever.

"Now take off your bra for me."

Swallowing her nervousness, Regan reaches with her right hand and pulls her left bra strap down at an agonizing pace. When Asha gestures with a wave of her fingers to continue, Regan repeats the action for the other strap with her left hand. She's about to reach behind and unhook when she considers a bolder choice and pulls the black cotton down first, exposing her breasts to Asha's approving nod. A moment later, she releases the garment and lets the material flutter to the floor, no longer relevant.

"You're getting the hang of this," Asha says, just loud enough to be heard. "Now take your hair and sweep it to one side for me. I want to see all of you, and that includes your neck. Has anyone ever told you how perfect your collarbones are, Regan? How it was a relief when you wore higher necklines to our meetings because I couldn't be distracted by the thought of kissing them?"

This is news to Regan. They'd met four or five times when Asha had been looking for a new apartment, but not once during those tours had there been any indication of something more. Asha hadn't even started flirting with her until the contracts had been drawn up.

Regan's fingers move unbidden to trace her own collarbones. Her eyelids close for a few seconds at the tickling sensation of her own touch, combined with the memory of Asha's mouth there before, how she'd bitten Regan with abandon.

"Now a little lower." Asha says.

Regan opens her eyes again as she complies. Her nipples have tightened in the cooler air and from the sound of Asha's voice. The first time Regan brushes them with tentative fingertips, she bites her bottom lip to keep from crying out.

"Stop that," Asha says a little harsher. "You will hold nothing back. I want to hear *every*. Single. Reaction. Clear?"

Regan nods and circles her nipples with her middle fingers. She doesn't hold back the happy sigh at the enjoyable sensation, and Asha gives one of her rare, encouraging smiles. She still seems quite unruffled despite watching with such intent. Regan senses a challenge in disrupting that poise and pinches her nipples between thumb and forefinger, surprising even herself with the gasp it draws out of her.

She's never been quite this sensitive before. The concentration seems to be helping.

"You've been so *good*, Regan, but there's something I need to know." Asha leans forward just a little, her knuckles straining as she grips the arms of the chair. "Are you wet?"

There's an obvious answer—Regan can already tell she's soaked. But Asha's words sound more like a clue than a simple question, so Regan trails one hand over her abs and toys with the waistband of her panties.

"You can't tell from there," Asha says, proving Regan's approach was the desired one. "Touch yourself, darling. And show me how wet you are."

Her mouth is dry in anticipation, so Regan licks her lips. She stops fiddling with the thin band of elastic and slips her hand beneath the cotton. She skims the tight curls and is unsurprised to find she's already wet there. By the time she passes over her clit, barely daring to touch it, her two fingers are already slick. She keeps the rest clasped in a half fist, not daring to assert more pressure yet. Regan moans as she drags her fingers back through the wetness before slipping her hand free once more and displaying it in the warm light of the room.

"Well." Asha sounds a little impressed. "It seems instruction works for you. I think it's time we lost the last of your clothes, don't you agree?"

Regan makes to take off her girl shorts, but Asha raises her hand.

"Not entirely. Just pull them down to about midthigh. I want to see you soaked for me, but putting a little restraint in place can't hurt for now. Trust me when I tell you we're going to be taking our time."

Nearly every muscle in Regan's body clenches. She yanks her underwear down.

"Now touch yourself again. Don't let that other hand get lazy. I'm sure your nipples are even more sensitive now." Asha runs her tongue along her teeth for a second. "Don't touch your clit yet. Anywhere else is permitted. Find a rhythm. Let me hear it."

It's a new task Regan attacks with enthusiasm. She rolls her nipple with less pressure than before, alternating with dragging her nails over each breast in turn, and it makes the moans bubble up even quicker. Her right hand, just a little bit stronger than her left, is put to good use between her thighs. Regan can't bring herself, even in her thoughts, to use more explicit terms for her own body. She thinks she might be able to if Asha demands it of her. It's exciting to have that confidence in what Asha can coax out of her.

Parting the lips with no resistance, Regan sinks two fingers inside herself. The relief of that first thrust makes her cry out. She's been aching inside since this started, a particular pull that's almost magnetic in her need to be touched there. Asha watches until that point. Just before Regan withdraws her fingers to stroke through her folds a little more, Asha snaps an order to stop.

Regan ceases all movement, as awkward as it is. With her own fingers inside her, her nipple pressed between thumb and finger, mouth open from the cry that just escaped her, chest heaving with labored breath, she looks to Asha for what comes next.

"Hold just like that." Asha pushes herself out of the chair and yanks her skirt back into place after it's ridden up on her hips. "I mean it. Don't move. I'm going to get a drink, and I expect to find you exactly like this when I return."

Asha clicks off toward the kitchen, still in her heels. Regan listens to her opening cupboards, retrieving a glass. There's a muttered curse before Asha finds the half-empty bottle of Scotch. To her surprise, Regan hears the fridge opening and Asha retrieving something from the freezer drawer. She doesn't usually drink Scotch on the rocks, but a moment later, ice rattles in the glass.

Regan could move a little. Release the pressure for a second and get right back to how she was. Only the instinct to rebel is absent. She feels better because Asha is completely in charge here, and Regan wants to do everything she asks.

When Asha returns, Regan beams with pride that she hasn't moved even a fraction of an inch.

Asha rolls her eyes. "Don't get smug. But that was very good. I'm impressed."

Regan looks at her, awaiting further instruction.

"Continue what you were doing before."

Asha doesn't return to her chair. One night of this and Regan already knows that chair will always belong to Asha.

Asha sinks her whisky in one mouthful, leaving the two small ice cubes in the glass. She hesitates for a moment before lifting the glass again and letting one slide into her mouth.

Her lips are cool when she kisses Regan, careful not to touch her in any other way. When Regan parts her lips to deepen the kiss, Asha presses the ice against her tongue and then pulls away.

"Use it." Asha takes her seat and crosses her legs once more. This time, though, she pulls off her shoes and tosses them aside. "Take the ice and draw me something."

Regan takes the ice cube from her mouth and holds it in front of her. Reluctantly, she slips her hand out from between her legs since Asha is changing the game. Uncertain, she draws a line across the top of her breasts with the ice, not expecting it to feel as shocking or as pleasant as it does.

"Oh!" She gasps.

Asha shushes her, finger against her lips. She sets the glass down, attention rapt on Regan. Regan takes the ice and starts beneath her ear, bold lines down her throat and then skimmed across the collarbones Asha likes so much. She lets the ice rest for a second in the hollows there before collecting it and swirling from the inside of her elbow down to her wrist.

She repeats the action on the other arm before rolling the cube across her stomach in curling designs that fade as soon as they're drawn, the trails of water absorbed by her skin. Her nerve endings are singing at the extra stimulation, and every time she looks at Asha to see her fixated on the movement of Regan's hands, the thrill increases.

The ice is melting fast. She drags it up over the curve of her breasts, circling the nipples as she did with her fingers not so long ago. When she presses the ice against the hard peaks, Regan bends forward with the strength of her body's reaction. It's like a lightning bolt pulling behind each nipple and her clit simultaneously. Asha gasps, wriggling a little in her chair.

When the ice is gone, Regan shows her empty hand to Asha and then continues touching herself in the same way.

"I've always wondered how you'd look doing this. Especially after those first couple of dates when you clearly wanted to take me home but settled for a kiss. Did you go home those nights and touch yourself, thinking about me?"

Regan's relieved she's not allowed to answer. She isn't sure she trusts herself.

"I really would like to watch that," Asha says. "But we'll try that another time. I'm no longer happy with you being out of reach. Do you want to touch me, Regan?"

That's not even a question. Regan nods, climbing down from her bed to stand in front of Asha.

"You've been patient," Asha says. "Now come sit on my lap without those." She motions for Regan's underwear to come all the way down.

Straddle Asha's lap? Regan can absolutely do that. She places her hands on Asha's shoulders to steady herself, crumpling the silk beneath her hands, still damp from the melted ice. They're so close it's almost impossible not to kiss Asha, but still Regan holds her position and waits.

"I still want you to fuck yourself," Asha says, her enunciation crisp, maximizing the effect it has on Regan. "Take those talented fingers and slip them inside. Not too fast, not at first, but make sure you really feel it."

Regan's hand is in motion before she's conscious of making the decision to do it.

"You have permission to touch your clit with the other hand. Go slow. Just gentle touches for now, darling."

There's a part of Regan that wants to know how Asha is doing this, how she can read Regan's body like an editorial and analyze every emotion running through it. Regan pushes down against her own fingers as she starts to thrust, and there's no doubting the effect on Asha as she bites her lip again. It's a little awkward using both hands at this angle, but Regan's flexible and willing to push through just about anything.

"Good girl," Asha whispers. Regan almost comes on the spot. Her moan must be a giveaway because Asha chuckles. "But you haven't earned the right to come yet. I'll give you permission to beg when it's time."

That's enough to make Regan light-headed, but her fingers don't miss a beat. She curves her back a little more to get the angle she really needs, her hair falling forward in dark waves and brushing Asha's face for a moment. She thinks Asha will scold her, but there's only a smile in response, Asha's eyes closing for a second in what might be bliss.

Regan couldn't keep quiet now if she tried, but she's careful not to let the sounds racing out of her form actual words. Mostly, it's ragged breaths, somewhere between sobs and sighs. Regan looks down at Asha's hands, now clutching the chair with a death grip.

As the thrusts of her fingers increase in pace and power, Regan moans right by Asha's ear, tickling her skin with her breath. She wants Asha to be pleased with her, wants Asha to be so turned on by Regan's actions that she gives in and touches her too. But she wants most of all to do what Asha told her. She'll wait for permission, no matter how close she already feels.

She almost falls over that edge with a particular twist of her fingers, combined with the featherlight pressure at her clit.

"Stop," Asha says. "Regan, stop."

Regan stills her movements, waiting and trying to catch her breath.

"You know now that you can do this and do it well." Asha lets go of the chair and runs her fingertips down Regan's spine. She arches back into the touch, hissing in pleasure. "You can shut out the world and take a moment for yourself."

It's not difficult to nod in agreement. Regan knows this is still new—they've only been together a matter of months—but already Asha has become a tether to reality for her. When so much of her life has been crazy, this part keeps making more sense.

"But for now." Asha reaches between Regan's thighs and pulls her hand free, making Regan groan at the loss. She's still pressing down on her clit, but Asha takes Regan's slick fingers and swipes them across a bare nipple like a brushstroke. She licks the wetness from Regan's nipple. Regan's close enough to coming that it's a miracle when she stops herself.

"Beg," Asha says when she's done sucking Regan's nipple until it's rock hard before doing the same with the other. She doesn't let go of her wrist the whole time.

Finding her voice, Regan is a little shocked by the torrent of words that spills out. "Please, God, please. Asha, I need…please, please let me come."

Asha guides Regan's fingers to her lips. She kisses the fingertips before sucking on them with unexpected tenderness. When she runs her tongue along the side of Regan's index finger, Asha's other hand brushes past Regan's fingers on her clit. For a moment, she mirrors the teasing flicks of her tongue with her finger, tracing the edges of Regan's entrance, but whether from impatience or Regan's muttered chant of "please" repeated over and over, Asha relents and thrusts two fingers inside.

Regan rubs her clit in earnest, and Asha adds a third finger. She stops toying with Regan's fingers and pulls her into an openmouthed kiss instead. When the kiss ends, there's almost no time for Asha to say, "Come, Regan," before she does.

And, oh, how she does.

Her whole body tenses, tuned to the vibration of Asha's movements and her own. Regan grasps blindly for Asha with her free hand, tugging at her hair and pulling her face against Regan's breasts as she rides out her orgasm. Asha licks and sucks at the sensitive skin as Regan cries out. Maybe it's a scream, but it's just noise and feeling, and everything is so, so bright until finally, finally she collapses against Asha.

"I think you needed that." Asha works her hand free and pulls Regan into something more like a hug. "You were so good."

"You made me good," Regan says when words come back to her, heavy and foreign on her tongue. She can hear nothing over their combined heartbeats, the slowing of their rapid breathing. If she closes her eyes, there's nothing but this moment, this safety and calm of being with Asha.

"Less stressed?" Asha asks, thumb stroking Regan's cheek.

"Yup." Regan laughs around the word. "In fact, I only have one concern." She opens her eyes again to look at Asha.

"What?" Asha frowns.

"I'm concerned that you haven't told me what you want me to do to you in return." Regan accepts a kiss in response, her smile blossoming under it.

"Get your breath back." Asha shifts under Regan and gives away her own unaddressed needs. "I have a few ideas."

Something Salty, Something Sweet

Emma Weimann

New England, Summer 2001

Vera Young sighed and wiggled her toes. A whirlpool was one of the finest inventions ever, especially if situated outside and far, far away from prying human eyes.

Being someplace where nobody demanded anything from her was just what she needed. The whiny cicada song had a mellow quality tonight, helping her to let go of all the shit that had happened at work these past weeks. She enjoyed how the water's warmth seeped into her bones and made her drowsy. Finding time to take a break was a luxury in her life, since there was no doubt she was an adrenaline junky. Being a partner in an international law firm was something she enjoyed but ever since meeting Maddy, her priorities had slightly shifted. Work wasn't everything anymore.

Maddy, whose legs were longer than Route 66 and whose tongue was sharper than the kitchen knives she used as a chef. Maddy, who had brought new joy and meaning to Vera's life. Maddy, who had planned something special for the first evening of their vacation.

Yes. Life was good.

Vera put her head back and closed her eyes, letting the memory of their afternoon together wander through her mind—the long walk, the wonderful picnic, the kissing... Thinking about the teenage-like foreplay they'd had in the car earlier made her horny. Well, hornier than she had already been.

Being able to enjoy the slow, dull pulse that bordered on an ache around her clit was wonderful—simply because she knew that later tonight she would enjoy slow sex, teasing sex, wonderful "let's take all the time in the world" sex. Making love with Maddy was fun. They had brought a bag full of Maddy's toys, some of which they'd never used before. The thought increased the pulse between Vera's legs. A lot.

"Hey." Maddy's soft voice caused a shiver of delight to run down Vera's back.

"Hey, yourself." She drank in the sight of the woman who had stolen her heart.

Dressed in blue jeans, a dark blue button-down shirt, and moccasins, Maddy looked as comfortable in her skin as any human being possibly could. She had aged more than well, and nobody guessed her to be in her mid-fifties. Maddy's gray hair accentuated light blue eyes that always reminded Vera of a perfect summer sky.

"It's time. You can come…inside," she said with a teasing smile, holding out a fluffy bathrobe and a towel.

A tingle raced through Vera. She knew that smile. It was a promise that made her dash out of the whirlpool and nearly fall over her own feet. "I'm really looking forward to see what my personal chef has come up with."

"It's only going to be a secret for a few more moments."

Maddy began to move the towel over Vera's back, her arms, her breasts, making her skin tingle and her insides melt.

Something warm unfurled in her belly and bloomed and spread between her thighs. "You're getting me all wet." Vera's voice sounded rough to her own ears.

"No, I'm helping you get dry."

"That is only true for certain parts of my body." She took the towel out of her lover's hands. As much as she enjoyed this… "If you don't stop we may not eat at all." She was hungry—for both sex and food. "Something makes me think that I need to stock up on energy."

"You may be right." Maddy's smile bordered on evil. "But we'll have a light dinner. Sex on a full stomach is no fun."

Vera sucked in a breath. "We'll have sex." In the most possible dramatic way she put a hand over her heart. "Oh, my."

"Only if you want to."

"If we must, we must." With a laugh, Vera put on the bathrobe.

They entered the cabin together, holding hands.

A whiff of something that smelled of herbs drifted through the air. Vera frowned. The dinner table in the living room was empty, except for the colorful flowers they had picked this afternoon. There were no candles, no soft music playing. Everything looked exactly as it had earlier.

"I want this evening to be something very special for you." There was a slight nervousness in Maddy's voice. She turned towards Vera, never breaking the physical connection between them. "And we'll start in the kitchen."

"You're so mysterious."

She chuckled. "I try my best."

Following Maddy into the kitchen, Vera breathed in the wonderful aromas. A bottle of white wine stood on the well-worn wooden table. Both glasses were already filled. But neither cutlery nor plates were in sight. This was really not at all what Vera had expected.

"Please sit down."

She didn't need to be asked twice, her stomach growling in anticipation. Maddy was an awesome chef.

"Not on the chair."

"But—"

"On the counter."

Vera stared at the counter. It had a stone top and surely would be an uncomfortable, cold place to sit.

"I adore you." Maddy stepped behind Vera and kissed her neck. "And tonight I want to pamper you…and turn you on at the same time." She nipped at an earlobe, before placing feather-light kisses on Vera's neck.

Vera's breathing quickened. "All right."

"We'll eat three courses and all of them contain ingredients that are known as aphrodisiacs." Another nip. This time a bit harder. "And I want to find out if the tales are true."

Shit. This was going to be one evening of sweet torture.

"Come on. I'll help you."

And then, for the first time in her life, Vera found herself on a kitchen counter, dressed only in a bathrobe. Her prim and proper friends would be scandalized.

Maddy put a glass of wine into her hand. "To you, to us, to this weekend, and to life together."

The words were perfect, as was the wine, which had a slight velvety taste.

"The first course was an easy decision." Maddy went to the oven and took out a tray. "The starter is steamed artichokes with lemon-pepper butter." She put the tray down on the counter, together with a basket of white bread, and a small dish filled with some kind of dip. "Did you know that in the Middle Ages women were forbidden to eat artichokes?"

Vera stared at the feast. The smell made her mouth water. "Really?"

"Yes, due to its aphrodisiac qualities." Maddy chuckled. "It was Catherine de' Medici who broke the gender barrier for us. She loved artichokes. And a king."

"I always liked her. Though I would have preferred for her to love a queen. She really missed out."

The skin around Maddy's eyes crinkled as she smiled.

Vera loved every single one of those wrinkles. They were sexy. Her lover was sexy and it didn't matter one bit that there was an age difference of over fifteen years and a lot of grey hair between them. "Come here."

Without hesitation Maddy closed the distance. There was nothing hurried or demanding about their kiss. It was tender, so very tender and promising.

Tracing her tongue around those soft lips, she cupped Maddy's face in one hand. A quiet moan was her reward. "I'll never get enough of you."

The air was charged between them and all Vera wanted was to skip the damn menu and drag her into the bedroom. They could eat later.

"I know exactly what you're thinking about."

Vera grimaced. "That obvious?"

"Yes." Her eyes shone.

"Would it be a bad idea?"

"Any other night, no. Tonight, yes."

"I think the food is working already and I haven't had one bite yet." She let her head fall onto Maddy's shoulder.

"Good. But how about giving it a try, first?" With a smile, Maddy picked a small artichoke up and dipped it into the lemon-pepper butter before holding it out to Vera. "Open your mouth."

She did and groaned. Heaven. This was heaven on her tongue. What a delicious taste, received from those long fingers that knew exactly how to comfort her, to guide her, to play her in the most intimate moments.

Out of reflex, she took Maddy's hand. Then she put those fingers against her mouth. One by one, she sucked in Maddy's index finger, her middle finger, and her ring finger, lathed them with her tongue, and gave each one a parting nip between her teeth.

"You're—" Maddy swallowed hard, "you're not supposed to lead tonight."

"Oh. All right." With a tinge of regret, Vera let go of her hand. "You're the boss."

"At least for now." She winked. "I do have plans for you tonight." With those words Maddy slowly opened the bathrobe.

Vera sucked in a breath as cool air hit her sensitive skin. With fascination she watched how her lover dipped a finger into the lemon-pepper butter and then coated one of Vera's nipples with the lukewarm butter, never breaking eye contact. Her fingertip circled the hardened nipple then darted across the top of the sensitive nub.

"Oh. . ." A glowing flow of heat was running through her blood.

The finger was replaced by a warm, wet tongue and Vera wanted to come right there on the counter. Her whole body pulsed. She ached to grind against Maddy, who chose that moment to break the contact and let go of the nipple.

"No!"

For a moment that felt like an eternity they didn't talk, the only sound filling the kitchen heavy breathing and the ticking of a clock on the wall.

"Yes, sweetheart. Slow. Remember, it's all about being slow tonight." Maddy brought her lips so close to Vera's that it was almost a kiss, but instead of closing the tiny gap that she had left between them, she said softly, "Slow."

"Bitch."

"Maybe, but I'm your bitch."

And there was that smile that Vera adored.

"The main dish won't take long. Why don't you lie down on the sofa and listen to some music. But no touching yourself."

Vera blinked. "You want to get rid of me?"

"On the contrary. But I need to focus on the next course before I invite you back."

Disappointment battled with curiosity. "Then help me down, please."

"It will be my pleasure, m'lady."

Vera walked out of the kitchen with the most provocative hip roll she was able to produce, taking her still half-full wine glass and Maddy's laughter with her. Her whole body was thrumming and she honestly wanted nothing more than to orgasm. But she had received orders. The question was, what else would Maddy serve—for dinner and later, after they had eaten the food?

With a sigh, she lay down on the sofa and closed her eyes. Her whole body was hot and the wetness between her thighs was nearly embarrassing. Sweet torture was probably the best description of what had happened so far.

"Are you relaxing?" Maddy called from the kitchen.

"Yes." She closed her eyes and tried to guess from the sounds exactly what was happening in there. Cutlery. The oven door. What would the second course bring? She sniffed the air. The aromas that were hitting her nose were spicy…maybe fish?

Footsteps approached the sofa.

She opened her eyes.

"Hey, stranger. Are you ready for the next course?"

"Yes." Vera took the outstretched hand and let herself be pulled up. "That was fast."

"It will still be a few minutes, but I didn't want to leave you alone for so long." Maddy planted a soft kiss on Vera's lips. "Have I told you lately how much I love you?"

"You have. I think in the few months we've been together, I've heard it more often than in the nearly fifteen years I was married to Peter."

"Stupid fool. And lucky me."

It wasn't often that Vera thought of her damn marriage anymore. She had been so unhappy, so alone, and so cruel to others back then. Her past had been a time of anger and bitterness, leaving her to think that happiness was a lie. Until Maddy had appeared and hugged the unhappiness right out of her. "You saved me."

"No," Maddy said. "You saved yourself."

Vera laughed. "Okay. You saved my employees."

"From the bitter witch?"

"Yes, from the bitter, wicked witch."

"I don't think I ever met her. All I met was a wonderful lady with very good taste in food and the nicest laugh I'd ever heard."

"You're delusional."

"No, but I fell in love the moment I saw you."

Vera produced an unladylike snort but otherwise kept quiet. For her, it had been a longer journey. Back then, she wasn't ready to trust anyone and had never thought that the person who would melt her heart and show her true love would be a woman. A woman who had courted the hell out of her.

An alarm went off in the kitchen.

"Ah, the next course is ready. Come on."

Maddy removed a tray of oysters from the oven. This time there were plates and cutlery on the kitchen table. Vera rubbed her brow. She loved oysters. She really did. But she had been looking forward to more foreplay on the counter, to those wonderful long fingers on her—and maybe in her. Eating the main course at the table was somehow… so mundane.

She sat down on a chair and this time Maddy didn't stop her. Well, all she could do was sit and wait for what would happen. She tried to keep the smile on her face while staring at the food.

"I'm sure you've already heard that oysters are considered an aphrodisiac." Maddy smiled down at her.

"Yes."

"One of the reasons is that they are slippery and sensual. Another is that they are able to change their sex from male to female and back."

That was indeed new to Vera. "So they can be male and female, not male or female?"

"Yes. It's said that oysters understand both the feminine and the masculine experience of love. I know how much you love them and that's why we're having New Orleans baked oysters tonight." She put a finger on Vera's nose. "By the way, this is a creole dish and full of delicious spices."

"How do you eat those?" She had only ever had them raw.

"I'll show you in a minute. But first you have to get up, please."

Ah. So there was something more creative to this course than baked oysters. Vera happily rose from her chair.

Maddy took the bathrobe's belt into her hand. "I think that you'll enjoy the oysters a lot." Her voice was low and sexy.

Vera shivered.

"But first things first." Maddy opened the belt and let Vera's bathrobe fall open. "So beautiful and mouthwatering."

Vera's breath quickened as, once again, the evening's cool air hit her skin.

"This time I need more skin." And with that, the bathrobe fell to the floor.

Standing naked in the kitchen before her fully dressed partner was not something Vera felt totally comfortable with. On the other hand, she couldn't deny how turned on she was and how much she wanted to be taken. Right here. Now.

But Maddy didn't touch her. "Sit down, please." She pointed at the table. "The main course is served and we don't want to eat it cold."

With a titanic effort, Vera didn't use the curse that was sitting on her tongue but instead carefully sat down, flinching slightly when her naked bottom hit the cold wood. It really was a good thing that this cabin was so secluded. Just the thought of someone walking in on them… Her, naked on a kitchen table. She couldn't contain her laughter.

"Hey. What is that about?"

"Can you—can you imagine if anyone saw us like this?"

Maddy smiled. "Oh, I can easily imagine how jealous most people would be."

Vera frowned.

"Do you know how many would love to change places with me?"

She could feel the blush on her face. "I don't think—"

"So many people don't even dare to fantasize. Right now, we're living a fantasy." With those words she leaned forward, carefully cupped Vera's breasts, and whispered in her ear, "I want you to know that I have a hard time coming up with reasons why we shouldn't skip right to dessert."

"Yes, why don't we?" Vera's stomach tightened in the most pleasant way.

"Patience, love. I want you to be so turned on for dessert that you can't think straight anymore."

With a wink, Maddy let go of Vera's breasts, picked up an oyster, and slurped it down in much the same way one did with the raw ones. Then she licked her lips, her eyes never leaving Vera's. "Delicious."

Vera bit her lip in an effort not to moan, barely resisting the urge to cross her legs to stifle the throbbing in between. This was cruel. Really, really cruel.

"It's your turn." A small smile. "With the oysters."

"You're lucky that I love you," Vera said with a shaky voice. Then she copied what Maddy had done. The oyster's texture was different but the spices didn't take away from the delicacy. They increased the fun and put fireworks on Vera's tongue. Just the way she liked it.

"And?"

Vera noticed the red tinge of Maddy's cheeks. To realize that she wasn't the only one being affected made her feel a lot more relaxed. "This is good." She slurped down another. "You've really done your best to pamper me tonight."

Maddy winked. "That's true. But we need to prove that these foods really are aphrodisiacs." She slowly brought her hand up and ran a finger over Vera's cheeks and lips. "So moist."

The kiss that followed was more of a brush. Vera got lost in the moment and in the touch.

Once more Maddy slowly broke their connection.

For a moment they just looked at each other. Vera took in the wonderful blue of her lover's eyes, the small scar on her upper lip, and the mischievous smile that was playing around that kissable mouth.

Then Maddy's hands were covering Vera's breasts and next her world was nothing but hands and lips and tongue on and in places that were never mentioned over the kind of dinners she usually had. In between they fed the oysters to each other until they were gone and Vera was a throbbing and whimpering, yet happy, mess. This was absolutely the most fun she'd ever had over shellfish.

"I really don't want to stop, but there is more to come." Maddy's full lips were parted as she took deep breaths.

As much as Vera wanted to kill Maddy for stopping once more, she was curious as to how this would continue. "I—" she cleared her throat. "I fear that whatever is coming next will kill me. Though I have no idea how you could top what you've already served."

"First of all, you have to stay undressed for the next course."

Vera lifted her eyebrows.

"Shall we relocate to the bedroom?" Maddy held out her hand.

"All right." Vera linked their fingers with Maddy's and followed, her knees weak. She had no idea what would come next. Well, dessert…usually. But how?

The bedroom was warm and the huge bed was empty, except for two cushions. The blanket sat on a chair close by.

A wave of excitement rushed through Vera. This looked really promising.

"Please stay here for a moment. I need to get something out of the other oven." With those words, Maddy disappeared.

There was a second oven?

It didn't take long for her to come back with a bowl full of something. "This is not dessert." She picked something out of the bowl. "Please open your mouth for me."

Vera did and groaned. The mixture of sweet and salty was like nothing she had ever tasted.

"Those are bacon-wrapped figs. Their harvest was celebrated by the ancient Greeks with a wild, sexy ritual. Figs are associated with fertility and while I don't expect you to carry my children after tonight…" she wiggled her eyebrows, "I liked the idea of the wild, sexy ritual a lot."

Vera took another one in her mouth, hand-fed by Maddy. It was as good as the first, if not better.

"When I was thinking about what to prepare for dinner, I immediately knew that I had to have these as part of the meal. Wanna know why?" Her voice had gone even deeper than usual.

Vera's heart raced faster. "Yes."

"They are salty and sweet and their taste reminds me of you when I lick you."

"Oh, God," Vera moaned. The fluttering in her stomach spread throughout her body and right into her pussy.

"And now I'll serve dessert but I'll be the one doing the eating." Maddy laughed, a low, throaty chuckle.

Vera's breath caught in her throat. She was shocked at how aroused she was. This wouldn't take long. Not at all.

Maddy stepped closer, wrapping her hands around both of Vera's wrists, their bodies ever so slightly touching. "I love you."

No matter how often she heard those words, she would never get tired of them. "I love you too."

Maddy pressed her soft lips against Vera's. The kiss started off light, tentative even, nearly innocent until Maddy coaxed Vera's mouth open, teasing tongue against tongue before withdrawing.

With shaky legs, Vera found a comfortable place on the bed.

"Now it's my turn." Within moments, Maddy's clothing was scattered across the carpet—button-down shirt, trousers, socks, panties, and bra, all tossed on one pile.

Vera couldn't help grinning as she leaned back. As much as she would have enjoyed a nice, slow striptease, realizing that she wasn't the only one who couldn't wait anymore to feel skin on skin caused a shiver of delight to run down her spine. Maddy was so beautiful. Breathing deeply, Vera let herself fall backward.

In two steps, Maddy was straddling her on the bed. She slowly ran her fingers up Vera's body, from hips to stomach to chest, letting her fingertips graze past her breasts and then went the whole way down again. "I love how you react to my touch." Her thumb slowly circled Vera's clit.

The place between her thighs was an ocean and the ache building inside her nearly made her forget her own name. She moaned and moved, trying to create more friction, more pressure, more anything.

Maddy's fingers dipped into her wetness, started moving slowly, providing shallow thrusts that made sure she wouldn't be able to make it more than thirty seconds without coming.

Vera trembled, her hand making a fist on the sheets.

"You're beautiful." Maddy stopped moving her fingers.

Vera opened her mouth to protest. Her heart was racing and her clit was aching and she needed—

"And now I'm going to taste and savour you. Just like I would with a really good dessert."

The first bold stroke of Maddy's tongue over Vera's throbbing clit nearly was her undoing.

Maddy stopped. "Not so soon. I want this to last a little bit longer."

Vera choked back something between a sob and a scream. "I hate you."

The only reply she got was laughter. Maddy continued stroking her clit with her tongue, but this time the touch was feather light, barely there, teasing her until she wanted to cry and beg.

Vera closed her eyes, bit her lip, and tried to regain her composure, without much success.

"I need more access, honey," Maddy said.

Not wasting a second, Vera curled her right leg over a strong shoulder.

"You taste so good." Maddy hummed while her hands pushed Vera's legs wider to give herself more room, before she started again, with a slow rhythm and a tortuously languid pace.

Whimpering and whining in bliss, Vera weaved her fingers into Maddy's hair and pulled her tighter against her. Within moments, she had lost track of everything in the world except Maddy's touch. "Please," she begged between labored breaths, half-afraid that Maddy was going to stop again.

Her hips involuntarily twitched forward, once, twice and her lover met each thrust willingly. The waves of pleasure crested and crested. And this time Maddy didn't stop.

Vera tumbled over the edge, an explosion in her brain, and a cry on her lips.

As if coming through a daze, she became aware that her legs were unlocked and Maddy's warm body was half on top of her.

Maddy pressed her lips to Vera's forehead. "So, so beautiful."

Vera opened her eyes. Maddy held a glass of water for her that seemed as if she'd magically produced from somewhere. She took several long sips before she was able to croak, "That... this evening…you are the most erotic, wonderful thing I have ever experienced."

Maddy wiped her mouth. "I have some more crazy ideas."

"Yes?"

"Yes." She kissed Vera, who tasted herself on Maddy's mouth. It really was a combination of something sweet and something salty, just like the bacon-wrapped figs had been.

Maddy pulled the blanket from the chair and motioned for Vera to get closer.

She did and leaned her head against Maddy's shoulder and the puffy pillow behind her. Maddy tightened her arm around Vera's waist and it didn't take long until Vera drifted in a state between sleep and wakefulness. She just needed a short break before she would show Maddy that two could play the teasing game.

Maddy pulled Vera tighter against her. "Will you marry me?" Her voice was a whisper, soft and full of desire.

"You…What?" Vera wasn't sure that she'd heard correctly. There was still the sound of waves in her ears from the mind-blowing orgasm she'd had only moments ago. And she was already half asleep, maybe—

"Will you marry me?" It came out in a rush. Maddy took a deep breath. "I know that I'm much older. And I'm aware that this will not in any way be legally binding. But I love you and I want to spend my life with you. I want to make you happy. And try out every aphrodisiacal food in the world with you."

Vera turned around in Maddy's arms. "You really want to marry me?" She couldn't believe it.

"Yes, ma'am."

"You, Maddy Fisher, are the most romantic person I have ever met in my life. And, yes, I will." She moved her hand between her lover's legs and found the wetness she had expected. "But only if I get the dessert this time."

∽∾∝∾∾

WORTH THE WAIT

Jae

Jill strode up the driveway with a bounce in her step and nearly skipped to her front door. She couldn't wait to break the good news to Crash. Since Crash had given up her studio apartment in Los Feliz last month to move in with her, she would get to tell her in person.

When she unlocked the door and stepped inside, Tramp didn't greet her with his tail going a mile a minute as he usually did. Had Crash taken him to the backyard to run him through the agility course?

Low grunts drifted over from the living room.

What the...? Jill put her car keys on the side table by the door and walked down the hall to see what was going on.

The sight that greeted her made her pause midstep.

Crash was doing pull-ups on the horizontal bar attached to the doorframe.

Her knees were bent and her legs crossed at the ankles, so she dangled with straight arms. With a controlled motion, she pulled herself up until her chin was above the bar. The muscles in her forearms rippled, and her well-formed biceps flexed. God, that impressive display of strength made Jill weak in the knees. Her gaze was drawn to Crash's tank top, which had hiked up, exposing her taut abdomen and her sexy belly button. The sweat-dampened fabric clung to her breasts and her athletic torso.

Jill's body warmed as if she were the one doing the pull-ups. She moistened her suddenly dry lips with her tongue as she imagined tasting Crash's salty skin and running her hands beneath the tank top to cup her small, firm breasts. "God, you're so sexy."

Only when Crash let go of the bar and lightly dropped to the floor did Jill realize she'd spoken out loud. "Oh, hey. You're back already." Wiping her hands on her cut-off sweatpants, Crash crossed the hall toward her. Her blue eyes, which seemed to glow against her flushed skin, pierced Jill with an intense gaze. "How did it go? Did they give you the 'don't call us, we'll call you' spiel?"

Jill shook her head. "Not this time. They decided on the spot."

"They did? So what did they say?" Crash waved her fingers. "Come on. Tell me."

"Well, let's just say soon you won't be the only woman in this household who gets to wear a uniform at work."

Crash stared at her. "You got the role?"

Jill beamed and nodded.

"Woo-hoo! I knew it! You'll be the sexiest arson investigator in the history of TV!" Crash closed the remaining space between them and held out her arms for a bear hug but then pulled back at the last second. "Uh, damn, I'm all sweaty."

"I don't care." Jill threw herself into Crash's arms and deeply inhaled her scent. Even though she had walked into the house minutes ago, being in Crash's arms was what really felt like coming home. "So you think you'll be able to stand working with me again?"

"Stand?" Crash pulled back to look at her. "I'll love it. Maybe they'll let me do all your fire stunts."

Jill loved seeing the excitement in Crash's eyes. What a difference from last year, when the mere thought of being set on fire had made Crash lose her lunch.

"Plus we'll be able to see each other during breaks in shooting," Crash said. "Just imagine all those quickies we'll be able to have in your trailer…" Her sensuous mouth curved into a crooked smile.

"Ha! You wish." But there was no conviction behind Jill's protest. After all, she vividly remembered the hot quickies in her trailer on the set of *Shaken to the Core* back when they hadn't been a couple and Jill had convinced herself it was just sex. Really mind-blowing sex.

When they finally let go of each other, Jill looked around. "Where's Tramp?"

"I asked Susana to dog-sit until tomorrow. I thought I could take you to your favorite restaurant to celebrate. Laleh said she'd reserve a table for us at seven."

Jill stared at her. "You had her reserve a table before you even heard from me? But you couldn't know I'd get the role."

"I knew," Crash said with a quiet confidence that warmed Jill deep inside. "I mean, I didn't know they'd decide on the spot, but there was never a doubt in my mind that you'd knock their socks off."

No one had ever believed in her like this. A lump in her throat prevented Jill from speaking, so she pulled Crash close again and kissed her.

The heat rolling off Crash enveloped her. Their bodies melted into each other. Jill poured all her love and gratitude into the kiss.

Crash trailed her hands up and down Jill's back, as if silently telling her that she understood what she tried to communicate. When she raked her fingers through Jill's short, pixie-cut hair and angled her so she could deepen the kiss, desire sparked through Jill, and their kiss grew more urgent.

The velvety glide of Crash's tongue against hers made Jill's body tingle in a decidedly non-MS kind of way. She curled her fingers into the damp fabric of Crash's tank top and drew their hips together.

Crash moaned into her mouth and kissed her with even more passion.

All of Jill's senses came alive, and she drank in Crash's heat, her scent, her taste. She broke the kiss to draw in a raspy breath and leaned against Crash to support her wobbly knees. After six months together, Crash knew exactly how to kiss her senseless. "Wow."

Crash breathed just as heavily. "Yeah. I'd say you should audition more often if you kiss me like that afterward, but I want you to stay with *Engine 27* for a long, long time." She brushed her lips over Jill's, more gently this time, and then tore herself away with obvious reluctance. "Be right back. I need a shower before we head to the restaurant."

Yeah, me too. A cold one. Jill watched her walk away, again admiring her athletic build and the lithe way she moved. God, she was one lucky woman.

The bathroom door clicked shut behind Crash, and it wasn't long before the sound of the shower drifted over. Jill imagined sudsy water sliding down Crash's firm breasts, her flat stomach, and her strong thighs.

Or I could join her for a really hot shower—and then take her to bed to celebrate.

She shook her head, but she knew better than to deny herself what she wanted. There would be times when the fatigue would hit her or other MS symptoms would flare up, making it impossible for her to make love to Crash, so she had learned to make the best of the good days.

Grinning, she pulled her cell phone from her pocket and typed out a quick message.

Hey, Laleh. I know Crash reserved a table for seven, but can we make it later?

She added a winking smiley face and sent off the message.

Laleh's reply arrived within seconds.

LOL. How about tomorrow, same time?

Jill chuckled. She should have known Laleh would understand. After all, she and her girlfriend, Hope, were still in the can't-take-our-hands-off-each-other stage too.

Perfect, Jill answered. She put the phone away and kicked off her shoes on the way to the bathroom. By the time she pulled open the door, she had flung her shirt off too.

Crash was in the shower, her back to Jill and her face lifted into the spray. The glass hadn't yet fogged up, so Jill saw rivulets of water cascading down Crash's leanly muscled back, the slight flare of her hips, and her tight ass. God, Crash's body was a piece of art, and Jill couldn't wait to run her hands over every inch of it.

She dropped the rest of her clothes on the bathroom floor and softly cleared her throat so she wouldn't startle Crash. "Need someone to wash your back?"

Crash swiveled her head around and wiped water from her eyes. "I'll never say no to that."

When Jill stepped into the shower, Crash turned down the temperature of the water to avoid making Jill's MS symptoms flare. Then she moved so the warm spray hit Jill too.

Jill pressed against Crash's back. The feeling of Crash's wet skin against her own made Jill's eyes flutter shut. Struggling for some self-control, she reached around her for the shower gel. The scent of peaches rose as she squeezed out a dollop. She worked up a lather by rubbing her hands together, slid her arms around Crash, and cupped her breasts, stroking them with her sudsy palms.

Crash sucked in a breath and arched into her. "Um, that's not my back."

"Are you complaining?" Jill whispered into her ear.

"Hell, no!" Crash turned in her arms, making their bodies slide against each other.

A moan escaped Jill, but she gripped the shower gel as Crash reached for it. "Me first."

Crash nodded and held still as Jill soaped up her shoulders.

Jill loved having a girlfriend who was confident enough to let her take the lead in their lovemaking. She ran her hands down Crash's strong arms, enjoying the contrast of soft skin over hard muscles, and then tenderly stroked the insides of her wrists before entwining their fingers for a moment.

Crash squeezed softly and looked up from where she had watched Jill's hands trail over her body.

Their gazes met and held. Crash's dazzling blue irises swirled with so much love and passion that it felt like a caress.

Jill raised one of Crash's hands to her lips and kissed it, then sputtered as she tasted soap.

They laughed together, and it lightened the intense mood.

Jill poured out a little more shower gel and soaped up the raised burn scar on the back of Crash's neck.

Crash shivered but let her touch wherever she wanted.

Jill smoothed the lather over Crash's back and her lean hips, tracing every bruise and every scrape from her stunt work as if they were marks of honor. Finally, she slid her hands lower and massaged Crash's firm ass.

Groaning with pleasure, Crash reached for her.

But Jill knew she'd lose all self-control if she let Crash touch her, so she stopped her. "Turn around."

When Crash did, Jill pressed herself against her slick, warm back.

They both moaned as Jill's hard nipples drew patterns through the suds trailing down Crash's shoulder blades.

Electric sensations sparked in Jill's belly. She glided her sudsy hands over Crash's collarbone and then down to the slope of her breasts. She circled her areolas, making Crash squirm and writhe to get her hands on her nipples.

Jill teased her for a few moments longer, then rubbed her fingers over the hard points.

"God, Jill!" Crash reached for the tile wall with both hands as if needing something to hold on to.

Her quiet groans and the erotic slide of their wet bodies against each other sent tingles through Jill. With one last squeeze of Crash's nipples, she moved on and dipped her hands lower.

Crash's six-pack tightened beneath her touch. She widened her stance in anticipation.

Jill combed her fingers through the wet curls at the apex of Crash's thighs, but instead of sliding her fingers between Crash's legs, she diverted her path at the last moment and smoothed her palms over her hips and the outside of her thighs.

Crash let out a frustrated groan. "You missed a spot." Her Texas drawl became more pronounced, as it always did when she was aroused.

"Oh, did I?" Jill swirled her fingertips up and down the silky inside of Crash's thigh but never ventured much higher.

With a low growl, Crash whirled around. In an instant, they had switched places, Jill now pinned against the tiles.

The way her stronger partner held her pressed to the wall sent a shiver of need down Jill's body.

"Yeah, you did," Crash said into her ear. "Normally, I'd let you find it on your own, but Laleh is waiting for us, so we'd better make this quick."

Jill shook her head, spraying Crash with droplets of water. "Nope. I sent her a text, telling her we'll be by tomorrow. For now, I want a much more…intimate celebration."

Surprise flashed across Crash's face and was quickly replaced with a sexy grin. "Ooh. If that's the case, let's see if I can find all your spots instead." She took some shower gel, ran her fingers slowly down Jill's breastbone, and traced the curve of one rib just beneath her breasts.

Languorous heat spread through Jill's body. She leaned in to Crash's touch but then covered the hand caressing her side with her own. "No."

Crash arched her eyebrows. "No? You don't want me to wash you?"

"I know cleanliness is next to godliness, but there's something else I want you to do to me."

Crash gave her a questioning look. "Anything. You know that. If you're exhausted from the audition and would rather have a massage—"

Jill interrupted her with a kiss. "I don't want a massage," she whispered against Crash's lips. "Remember what we talked about when you helped me with my injections for the first time? That's what I want."

For a moment, Crash's face was blank, then the bottle of shower gel slid from her grasp and dropped to the shower floor. "You want me to…?" She cleared her throat.

"Use the strap-on." Jill knew Crash had one; she'd seen the harness in one of the boxes when Crash had moved in. Ever since then, she had wanted to try it out. They had even gone out to buy a new dildo together—one that appealed to Jill in shape and size. But while getting used to living with each other, preparing for the audition, and dealing with fatigue, the timing had never been right, so they hadn't used it yet. But now… She searched Crash's face. "Unless you're not in the mood."

Instead of a verbal reply, Crash dipped her beneath the spray to rinse off the suds, then quickly shut off the shower and shoved open the glass door.

Jill chuckled and stepped into the towel Crash held open for her.

They toweled each other off, and Crash chased down all remaining droplets of water with her lips, kissing them away.

By the time Crash took her hand and led her to the bedroom, Jill's legs already felt like gelatin. She'd never been so glad that they had moved the bedroom they shared downstairs into her former office.

Crash moved with purpose, striding to the dresser and opening the bottom drawer.

As she bent and rummaged through the drawer, Jill's gaze was drawn to her taut ass. A sudden vision of digging her fingers into those firm buttocks as Crash thrust into her flared through her mind. A little gasp escaped her, and she squeezed her thighs together.

Crash turned. She looked at the black leather harness in her hand, then raised her gaze to search Jill's face. "Are you sure this is what you want? It can get pretty… energetic."

Jill flashed a grin. "Energetic sounds great. Don't get me wrong. I love it when we make love slow and sweet. But every once in a while, I just want you to take me."

A groan tore from Crash's throat. "Jesus, Jill. I want that too. But if it becomes too much and you want to stop at any point…"

Jill took a step forward, right into Crash's personal space. She closed her fingers over Crash's that white-knuckled the harness. "I love how gentle and considerate you are." She whispered a soft kiss onto Crash's full lips. "But please don't treat me like I'm fragile. I get enough of that at work when directors don't trust me to do even the easiest stunts myself. I don't want you to think of me like that. I want to be desired."

"You are," Crash said immediately, her voice husky and her gaze intense. "I've never wanted anyone as much as I want you."

The raw desire in her eyes made Jill's head swim. She kissed Crash, this time more firmly. "Then put that thing on and show me."

"Why don't you put it on me?" Crash said, her usual confidence back in her voice.

God, that was hot. Jill took the harness from her, glad she was having a good day with no numbness or tingling in her hands. It took a few seconds for her to sort out where each strap was supposed to go. Once she had figured it out, she knelt and held out the harness for Crash to step into.

Jill then pulled the leather straps up her muscular legs, sliding her palms over her warm skin as she went. She traced a line along the straps that looped underneath

Crash's butt cheeks and stroked her index finger along the crease where Crash's thigh met her pelvis.

Crash shuddered.

"Remember when we first met and you helped me remove the stunt harness?" Jill asked. "That's what you did to me. Just one touch and I wanted you, even back then."

Crash pulled her up and kissed her, sliding her tongue along Jill's.

When the kiss ended, Jill was dazed with pleasure. "Where's…?"

Crash pressed the dildo into her hand before she could finish the question. "Do you still think this is okay? Size-wise, I mean."

Jill slid her fingers over the smooth, blue-and-white-marbled silicone, making Crash groan as if she could feel her touch as it glided over the toy. The dildo they had chosen wasn't too thick or too long, but it wasn't too small either. Jill's entire body was already tingling with the anticipation of having it inside her. "It's perfect," she whispered against Crash's lips. "And so are you."

Their lips came together with just the right mix of tenderness and urgency.

Gasping, Jill broke away, trailed the toy down Crash's taut belly, and slid it through the O-ring. With slightly unsteady fingers, she fastened the buckles on Crash's trim hips, then tightened the leg straps.

The dildo rode low on Crash's pelvis, jutting out at a slight upward curve.

Jill had expected it to look strange, maybe even a little silly, but on Crash, who stood with a confident stance, it looked hot. She reached out and smoothed her hand along the dildo, pushing it against Crash in the process.

Crash moaned and clamped her teeth onto her bottom lip as if she struggled for control.

Jill looked into her eyes. "Can you feel that?"

"Yeah." Crash's voice was husky and her pupils so wide that only a thin ring of her dazzling, ice-blue irises remained. "The flared base rubs against my clit if you do that."

"This?" Jill closed her fist around the toy and pumped once.

Crash surged against her. "God, yes."

"Good. I want this to be good for you too."

A helpless chuckle escaped Crash. "Oh, you definitely don't have to worry about that." She grasped Jill's hips with both hands, kissed her with an intensity that made Jill lightheaded, and walked her backward until they reached the bed, never breaking the kiss as she eased her down on it.

The sheets were cool against Jill's back, and she shivered in the air-conditioned bedroom, but her body instantly warmed as Crash followed her down, covering her with her familiar, solid weight.

The toy pressed against Jill's belly, trapped between their bodies. For a moment, Jill expected the unfamiliar feeling to throw her off, but instead, it ratcheted up her desire. It wasn't the strap-on itself that turned her on; it was that Crash wore it.

But Crash didn't seem in any hurry to use it. She took her sweet time, trailing kisses across Jill's cheek, along her jawline, and down the column of her neck.

Jill wove her finger into Crash's short, black hair as those talented lips moved lower.

Crash cupped one breast in her palm and gazed at it as if it were a piece of art. "You're so beautiful." Before Jill could answer, Crash lowered her head and painted circles around her taut areola with her tongue.

Ripples of delight shot across Jill's skin. She clutched at Crash's head, drawing her closer.

Crash licked the nipple—once, twice—then sucked it into her mouth.

A hot jolt surged through Jill, straight to her core. She cried out. Her hips arched off the bed, making her keenly aware of the dildo sandwiched between them. She writhed against Crash, who used her lips, her tongue, and her teeth to tease her nipple into a hardened point.

"Crash." She ran her hands down Crash's muscular back, then tugged on her hips, desperate for some friction.

"Not yet," Crash whispered against the damp skin of Jill's breast, making her shudder. "Relax. Enjoy." She moved to the other breast and lavished the same attention on it until Jill felt as if she were melting from the inside out.

"God, Crash. Please."

Leaning up on one hand, Crash reached between them with the other and rubbed the toy against Jill's wetness.

Every nerve ending in Jill's body seemed to come alive. She ground herself against the length of the dildo.

Crash covered Jill's mouth with hers, swallowing her moan, and kissed her, first tender, then long and hard. Finally, she broke the kiss, her breathing already ragged. "Now?"

Jill's entire body throbbed with need. "Yes."

With a trembling hand, Crash reached into the drawer of the bedside table and pulled out a small bottle.

Jill laughed shakily. "I don't think we need that."

"You can never have too much lube." Crash grinned. "I want this to feel good."

"It already does." She watched, transfixed, as Crash squeezed out a generous amount of lube and stroked her hand down the dildo. "God, that's hot."

Crash looked up, her gaze smoldering. She braced herself with one hand next to Jill's shoulder.

Both reached between their bodies at the same time. Their fingers brushed on the toy, and their gazes locked.

God. Jill hadn't known this could be so intimate.

Together, they positioned the tip of the dildo at her opening.

Crash's whole body was taut against hers. Jill felt Crash's pulse hammering as hard as her own.

Need spiraled through Jill. "Put it inside me." She groaned. "I need to feel you."

Crash echoed her groan. She watched Jill's face as she carefully eased the lube-covered dildo inside her an inch.

Jill's breathing hitched.

Crash stilled immediately. "You okay?"

"Very okay." She clutched Crash's back with both hands. "Keep going."

Crash tilted her hips forward and sank deeper inside with agonizing slowness, making Jill feel every inch of the dildo, until their hips were flush together.

Jill's mouth dropped open in a silent gasp. God. So good.

"Jill," Crash whispered, a note of awe and barely controlled hunger in her voice. She dropped her forehead against Jill's but otherwise held very still, giving Jill time to adjust to the fullness inside of her. "Too much?"

"No. Perfect." She loved feeling Crash against her…in her like this, loved seeing in Crash's eyes how much this turned her on too.

Crash dipped her head and kissed Jill's neck without moving her hips.

Jill gasped as Crash's teeth raked the sensitive spot beneath her ear. She pushed up against her with her hips and moaned as the dildo pressed even deeper.

Keeping their gazes locked, Crash placed her hands on either side of Jill and started to move inside of her in little back-and-forth strokes. She kept her pace gentle and steady. "God, I love this. I love you."

A shudder of arousal went through Jill. "Me too," she managed to groan out. Her ability to form a halfway coherent sentence was slipping away quickly.

Still moving against her in a leisurely rhythm, Crash caressed one breast and flicked her tongue over the other.

The added stimulation and Crash's achingly slow pace drove Jill crazy. She rocked against her, searching for more of the delicious pressure.

Crash withdrew partway, then filled her just as slowly, ratcheting up both Jill's pleasure and frustration.

Jill thrust forward to prolong the contact.

A strangled moan told her that she'd pushed the dildo against Crash. The steady rhythm faltered for a moment, and heat flared in Crash's eyes. A sheen of perspiration glistened on her handsome face. The muscles beneath Jill's hands quivered with the effort to hold back.

But Jill didn't want her to rein herself in. She rasped her fingernails down Crash's strong back, wrapped her legs around Crash's hips, and pulled her deeper. "Please, Crash. Don't hold back. Fuck me hard."

With a low noise that sounded almost like a growl, Crash dropped onto her forearms and began to thrust harder and faster.

Each long, deep stroke sent waves of pleasure through Jill. Watching Crash lose all control excited her even more. "God, yes. So good." She arched up against her, matching her stroke for stroke and losing herself in the rhythm they created together.

Crash's muscles flexed as she worked hard to please her. They both panted hard.

Their mouths connected in a wild kiss, tongues sliding against each other in the same urgent rhythm.

After a few heartbeats, Crash pulled away so she could watch her as she withdrew until she was barely inside, then pressed in again.

Jill surged against her with a sharp cry. She raked her nails down Crash's back and grabbed her thighs, her ass, desperately pulling her harder into her wet center.

An almost feral noise escaped Crash. She rotated her hips, angling the dildo up just right, hitting a spot that instantly reduced Jill to an incoherent mess.

"Oh my fucking God!" Jill's vision blurred. She knew she wouldn't last. Breathless gasps escaped her. Close. So close. She strained against Crash and tightened her legs around Crash's hips.

The next thrust made her eyes roll back in her head. Her movements lost all coordination, and all she could do was cling to Crash. She flung her head back into the pillow. Her eyes fluttered closed, her entire being focused on the amazing feeling gathering deep inside of her.

Crash let out a low groan and nipped Jill's exposed throat. "Jill. Look at me, Jill."

Jill dragged open her heavy lids. Their gazes connected.

Crash slipped one hand between them and stroked Jill's swollen clit.

White-hot pleasure seared through Jill. She tried to hold off, to prolong this incredible feeling, but as Crash snapped her hips forward again, it became a losing battle. Her inner muscles contracted around the dildo as her orgasm ripped through her. A guttural scream wrenched from her throat. She arched up one last time, then collapsed back onto the bed.

Crash slowed her thrusts but kept moving gently, drawing out Jill's climax.

As the last ripples of ecstasy faded away, Crash stilled and buried her face against Jill's throat. Her ragged breathing fanned over Jill's damp skin. "God, Jill," she whispered into the crook of her neck.

Every muscle in Jill's body was still languid with pleasure. Weakly, she lifted her hand and combed her fingers through Crash's short hair, which was damp from their shower and sweat.

Crash shuddered against her. After a while, she carefully withdrew.

Another flutter of sensation quivered through Jill, making her moan again.

Crash kissed her gently, then rolled off to lie beside her and held her close, with the dildo nestled between them, digging into Jill's side. Her skin was flushed and glistened with sweat. Her heartbeat thundered against Jill's chest.

"You didn't come, did you?" Jill asked when her brain started working again.

"Almost." Passion lit up Crash's blue eyes, making them seem to glow. "God, just watching your face while I moved inside you almost drove me over the edge at one point."

"Mmm, let's see if we can do something about that *almost*." Jill rolled her eager partner onto her back, settled at her side, and leaned over her.

The dildo jutted up between them, quivering with each of Crash's unsteady breaths.

"Let me take this off." Crash fumbled with the buckles of the harness.

Jill covered her hand with her own. "Wait. Let me."

Crash dropped her hands to the mattress and lay still, open to Jill's touch.

The way she gave up control was just as hot as watching her take it earlier had been.

Jill slid her hand down Crash's belly. The sweat-dampened skin felt as smooth as silk beneath her fingertips. She lowered her head to taste the perspiration glistening between Crash's breasts, then let her lips and her tongue follow the path of her hand down.

Crash's six-pack contracted under her touch, and her breathing sped up.

The scent of Crash's arousal filled her nostrils as she kissed a trail down her belly. "Jesus, Jill." Crash dug her hands into Jill's hair. "What are you...?"

Her words ended in a drawn-out groan when Jill slid her hand lower and ran it over the glistening silicone, grinding the base of the dildo against Crash. "Loving you." Jill pumped her hand again.

Crash arched up against her. "Careful. I'm not going to last if you...God...keep that up."

As sexy as the thought of getting Crash off like this was, Jill wanted more. She wanted to touch her. She trailed her fingers lower and slipped them beneath the warm leather of the harness, immediately encountering Crash's wetness.

Crash sucked in a sharp breath. She reached up to grip the headboard, her athletic body tightening beneath Jill.

Renewed need swirled through Jill, and she wanted the strap-on gone so she could get her mouth on Crash. Her hands flew to the buckles. Her fingers were a little unsteady now, so she fumbled for a moment before she managed to unfasten the buckles and eased the harness down Crash's quivering legs.

As it dropped to the floor, she trailed kisses along the curve of Crash's hips, where the buckles had left light marks on her skin, and then ran the tip of her tongue down one powerful thigh.

Crash let go of the headboard and parted her legs in silent invitation. Her hands roamed Jill's shoulders, up the back of her neck, into her hair. She dug her heels into the mattress, pushing herself upward toward her mouth. "Please."

Jill took hold of her hips and dipped her head down. She nuzzled into Crash's damp curls and breathed in her musky scent. Then, not wanting to make Crash wait any longer—unable to wait any longer herself—she slid her tongue through her wetness.

"Fuck!" Crash arched up against her.

Jill felt how close Crash was. She swirled her tongue through her folds and flicked it along one side of her clit. Crash's gasps and groans urged her on. Jill gripped her bucking hips more tightly and drew her closer, unable to get enough.

Crash's fingers tightened in her hair, and she breathed out her name like a plea or a prayer.

Jill closed her lips over her clit and sucked once, hard.

With a raw shout, Crash surged up against Jill's mouth one last time. Her legs clamped around Jill's head, then went limp. Crash dropped back onto the bed, her fingers still in Jill's hair.

Jill placed a soft kiss on Crash's swollen folds, making her twitch, then wiped her mouth and slid up Crash's damp body, enjoying the erotic feeling. One of her legs came to rest between Crash's thighs, which caused another low moan.

Crash blinked open her eyes and stared up at her, dazed. When Jill wanted to roll off to move onto her side, she wrapped her arms around her and held her in place.

Slowly, their erratic breathing settled down, and the drumming heartbeat beneath Jill's ear calmed along with her own.

Crash cradled Jill's face between her palms and kissed her. "God, you are incredible."

"Me?" Jill melted against her. "You did most of the hard work."

Crash shook her head. "That wasn't work. That was pure pleasure."

Jill hummed her agreement. "Oh yeah. It was quite the celebration. Why on earth did we wait so long to take that strap-on out for a test-drive?"

"Because good things are worth the wait." Crash's lips quirked into a crooked smile, but something in her eyes let Jill know she was talking not just about the amazing sex they'd just had but about their relationship in general.

Jill kissed the cute dimple in Crash's chin, then her soft lips. "Thanks for not giving up on me."

"Never," Crash said fiercely.

After one last, long kiss, Jill settled down with her head on Crash's shoulder and one arm and leg across her body while Crash held her. "Crash?" she said against her skin after a while.

"Hmm?"

Jill hesitated, but she knew it was silly, especially after what they had just done. She could ask Crash anything. "Have you ever…been on the receiving end of a strap-on?"

Crash stilled beneath her, no longer even breathing. "No, never." It came out as a husky whisper. She cleared her throat. "Is that something you would be interested in? Wearing the harness?"

"Mm-hmm. I'd really like to know what you felt the moment you pushed into me."

A groan tore from Crash's throat. "Jesus. Are you trying to kill me?"

"Only in a good way." Jill leaned up on one hand so she could study Crash's face. "If that's not something you're into, that's totally okay. I don't need toys to have a good time in bed with you, and I doubt I'd have the same energy and control you did anyway, but I thought…maybe you could be on top and ride me. God, that would be hot."

Crash groaned again and fanned herself. "Oh yeah. I'm definitely up for trying that with you."

"Really?"

"Sure. Anytime."

Jill grinned. "Great. Well, maybe not right now. You wore me out." She kissed Crash's shoulder and rested her cheek there for a minute, until she realized it was sticky with perspiration—and so was she. "I think we need another shower."

Crash's laughter vibrated through her. "Yep, we sure do. Then let's go take one. But this time, I get to wash you."

∞

If you enjoyed this short story, check out *Just Physical* by Jae, the novel in which Jill and Crash met and fell in love.

ABOUT THE AUTHORS

Lee Winter

Lee Winter is an award-winning veteran newspaper journalist who has lived in almost every Australian state, covering courts, crime, news, features and humour writing. Now a full-time author and part-time editor, Lee is also a 2015 and 2016 Lambda Literary Award finalist and has won several Golden Crown Literary Awards. She lives in Western Australia with her long-time girlfriend, where she spends much time ruminating on her garden, US politics, and shiny, new gadgets.

Jess Lea

Jess Lea lives in Melbourne, Australia, where she started out as an academic before working in the community sector. She loves vintage crime fiction, the writings of funny women, and lesbian books of all sorts. Jess can be found writing in cafes, in parks, and in her pyjamas at home when she should be at work.

A.L. Brooks

A.L. Brooks was born in the UK but currently resides in Frankfurt, Germany, and over the years she has lived in places as far afield as Aberdeen and Australia. She works 9–5 in corporate financial systems and her dream is to take early retirement. Like, tomorrow, please. She loves her gym membership, and is very grateful for it as she also loves dark chocolate. She enjoys drinking good wine and craft beer, trying out new recipes to cook, and learning German. Travelling around the world and reading lots and lots (and lots) of books are also things that fight for time with her writing. Yep, she really needs that early retirement.

Harper Bliss

Harper Bliss is a best-selling lesbian romance author. Among her most-loved books are the highly dramatic French Kissing and the often thought-provoking Pink Bean series. She is the co-founder of My LesFic, a weekly newsletter offering discount deals on lesbian fiction.

Harper lived in Hong Kong for 7 years, travelled the world for a bit, and has now settled in Brussels (Belgium) with her wife and photogenic cat, Dolly Purrton.

Emma Weimann

Emma Weimann knew at an early age that she wanted to make a living as a writer. She knew exactly how and where she wanted to write the books that would pay for her house at the beach and the desk with a view of the ocean.

Even though she has had those dreams for over thirty years now, neither the house nor the desk exist. Not yet. But she's making a living producing books, not just as a writer but also as a publisher, establishing Ylva Verlag and its international pendant, Ylva Publishing, in 2011 and 2012.

She also is the author of *Heart's Surrender*, a 2015 Golden Crown Literary Award Winner for lesbian erotica.

KD Williamson

KD is a Southerner and a former nomad, taking up residence in the Midwest, east coast, and New Orleans over the years. She is also a Hurricane Katrina survivor. Displaced to the mountains of North Carolina, she found her way back to New Orleans, where she lives with her partner of ten years and the strangest dogs and cats in existence.

KD enjoys all things geek, from video games to super heroes. She is a veteran in the mental health field, working with children and their families for more than ten years. She found that she had a talent for writing as a teenager, and through fits and starts, fostered it over the years.

Alison Grey

Alison has been writing since the age of ten. Her first works were poems and short stories; then she wrote her first novel-length book when she was eleven. It was a *Star Trek: The Next Generation* fanfiction.

In addition to writing, Alison likes spending her spare time with her friends. The vegetarian also loves cooking and baking. If she's got enough time, she reads books about history and about social and political sciences.

Lola Keeley

Lola Keeley is a writer and coder. After moving to London to pursue her love of theatre, she later wound up living every five-year-old's dream of being a train driver on the London Underground. She has since emerged, blinking into the sunlight, to find herself writing books. She now lives in Edinburgh, Scotland, with her wife and three cats.

Jae

Jae grew up amidst the vineyards of southern Germany. She spent her childhood with her nose buried in a book, earning her the nickname "professor." The writing bug bit her at the age of eleven. Since 2006, she has been writing mostly in English.

She used to work as a psychologist but gave up her day job in December 2013 to become a full-time writer and a part-time editor. As far as she's concerned, it's the best job in the world.

When she's not writing, she likes to spend her time reading, indulging her ice cream and office supply addictions, and watching way too many crime shows.

OTHER BOOKS FROM YLVA PUBLISHING

www.ylva-publishing.com

Breaking Character

Lee Winter

ISBN: 978-3-96324-113-0
Length: 315 pages (106,000 words)

Life becomes a farcical mess when icy British A-lister Elizabeth and bright LA star Summer try to persuade an eccentric director they're in love to win Elizabeth her dream role—while convincing a gossiping Hollywood they're not. Worse, they're closeted lesbians who don't even know the other is gay.

A lesbian celebrity romance about gaining love, losing masks, and trying to stick to the script.

A Curious Woman

Jess Lea

ISBN: 978-3-96324-160-4
Length: 283 pages (100,000 words)

Bess has moved to a coastal town where she has a job at a hip gallery, some territorial chickens, and a lot of self-help books. She's also at war with Margaret, who runs the local museum with an iron fist. When they're both implicated in a senseless murder, can they work together to expose the truth?

A funny, fabulous, cozy mystery filled with quirkiness and a sweet serve of lesbian romance.

Write Your Own Script

A.L. Brooks

ISBN: 978-3-96324-156-7
Length: 248 pages (87,000 words)

Beloved famous British actress Tamsyn Harris works hard to keep her career alive, which means hiding that she's a lesbian from the world. The last thing she expects at a retreat is to meet Maggie Cooper, an alluring author and fan who makes her question whether it might be worth risking everything for love.

A sizzling lesbian romance about finding out what's important in life.

Heart's Surrender

Emma Weimann

ISBN: 978-3-95533-183-2
Length: 305 pages (63,000 words)

Neither Samantha Freedman nor Gillian Jennings are looking for a relationship when they begin a no-strings-attached affair. But soon simple attraction turns into something more. What happens when the worlds of a handywoman and a pampered housewife collide?

Can nights of hot, erotic fun lead to love, or will these two very different women go their separate ways?

Drawing the Line

KD Williamson

ISBN: 978-3-96324-105-5

Length: 254 pages (85,000 words)

Pediatric resident Dani Russell is focused on her career and there's no room for anything else. Since her last relationship imploded, she's icy to almost everyone.

Detective Rebecca Wells is on a mission to fix her personal life. That means reaching out to her ex, Dani, to make amends. But is it too late?

An enemies-to-lovers, second-chance lesbian romance that's both powerful and sexy.

Contract for Love

Alison Grey

ISBN: 978-3-96324-086-7

Length: 301 pages (97,000 words)

Sherry lives in a trailer park with her son, trying to make ends meet.

Madison's life couldn't be more different. Her only goals are partying and bedding women.

When her grandmother threatens to disinherit her, Madison has to find a way to prove that she's cleaned up her act.

After a chance encounter with Sherry, Madison comes up with a crazy idea: she wants Sherry to play her fake girlfriend.

Major Surgery

Lola Keeley

ISBN: 978-3-96324-145-1
Length: 198 pages (69,000 words)

Surgeon and department head Veronica has life perfectly ordered...until the arrival of a new Head of Trauma. Cassie is a brash ex-army surgeon, all action and sharp edges, not interested in rules or playing nice with icy Veronica. However when they're forced to work together to uncover a scandal, things get a little heated in surprising ways.

A lesbian romance about cutting to the heart of matters.

Not the Marrying Kind

Jae

ISBN: 978-3-96324-194-9
Length: 314 pages (113,000 words)

Small-town florist Ashley loves creating wedding bouquets. Her own love life is far from blossoming since she's stuck in the closet.

Sasha isn't faring much better. Her bakery keeps her too busy for romance anyway.

When the town's first lesbian wedding forces them to work together, Sasha is soon tempting more than just Ash's sweet tooth.

What else is on the menu in this delicious lesbian romance?

Laid Bare – A Collection of Erotic Lesbian Stories
© 2019

"Flashbang" © 2015 Lee Winter
"A Different View" © 2018 Jess Lea
"Executive Dining" © 2019 A.L. Brooks
"58 Seconds" © 2019 Harper Bliss
"Help Yourself" © 2019 Emma Weimann
"Erasing the Lines" © 2018 KD Williamson
"Houseshare" © 2019 A.L. Brooks
"It's Getting Hot in Here" © 2019 Alison Grey
"Stress Management" © 2019 Lola Keeley
"Something Salty. Something Sweet" © 2016 Emma Weimann
"Worth the Wait" © 2019 Jae

ISBN: 978-3-96324-214-4

Also available as e-book.

Published by Ylva Publishing, legal entity of Ylva Verlag, e.Kfr.

Ylva Verlag, e.Kfr.
Owner: Astrid Ohletz
Am Kirschgarten 2
65830 Kriftel
Germany

www.ylva-publishing.com

First edition: 2019

Credits
Edited by Miranda Miller, Lee Winter, Amanda Jean, Jove Belle, Andi Marquette, and R.G. Emanuelle
Cover Design by Streetlight Graphics

Printed by
booksfactory
PRINT GROUP Sp. z o.o.
ul. Ks. Witolda 7-9
71-063 Szczecin
Poland
tel./fax 91 812-43-49
NIP/USt-IdNr.: PL8522520116